"Why
brushing
life for me?

Her body was instantly suffused with warmth, her pulse raced, and her heart began pounding. Nick's eyes seemed to reflect the rich, deep green of the forest and flicker with golden flames that hypnotized her. His touch was mesmerizing, and she was captured in a spell she hoped would never be broken.

"Tell me why you did it, Tracy," Nick asked again.

She lowered her eyelids, not sure what to say. Could she tell him the truth?

"Look at me, Tracy," he said, and she could not refuse him.

When she opened her eyes, the impact of their brilliant blue took his breath away. "You're so beautiful," he whispered.

It was more than she'd ever dared hope for, and now that she heard him say she was beautiful, she hardly dared believe it. She parted her lips for his kiss, her eyes never leaving his. . . .

WHAT ARE *LOVESWEPT* ROMANCES?

They are stories of true romance and touching emotion. We believe those two very important ingredients are constants in our highly sensual and very believable stories in the *LOVESWEPT* line. Our goal is to give you, the reader, stories of consistently high quality that may sometimes make you laugh, sometimes make you cry, but are always fresh and creative and contain many delightful surprises within their pages.

Most romance fans read an enormous number of books. Those they truly love, they keep. Others may be traded with friends and soon forgotten. We hope that each *LOVESWEPT* romance will be a treasure—a "keeper." We will always try to publish

*LOVE STORIES YOU'LL NEVER FORGET
BY AUTHORS YOU'LL ALWAYS REMEMBER*

The Editors

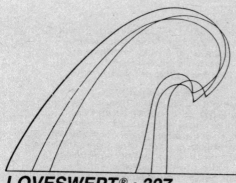

LOVESWEPT® • 327

Gail Douglas
Lost in the Wild

BANTAM BOOKS
NEW YORK · TORONTO · LONDON · SYDNEY · AUCKLAND

LOST IN THE WILD
A Bantam Book / May 1989

If you would be interested in receiving protective vinyl
covers for your Loveswept books, please write to this address
for information:

Loveswept
Bantam Books
P.O. Box 985
Hicksville, NY 11802

ISBN 0-553-21999-5

Published simultaneously in the United States and Canada

Bantam Books are published by Bantam Books, a division
of Bantam Doubleday Dell Publishing Group, Inc. Its trademark, consisting of the words "Bantam Books" and the
portrayal of a rooster, is Registered in U.S. Patent and
Trademark Office and in other countries. Marca Registrada.
Bantam Books, 666 Fifth Avenue, New York, New York 10103.

PRINTED IN THE UNITED STATES OF AMERICA

O   0 9 8 7 6 5 4 3 2 1

To Poppa and Lauri.
Thanks for falling off the trail bike "only twice."

One

Tracy Carlisle's glance swept over the guests assembled in the ballroom of her grandfather's sprawling Chicago mansion as she willed herself to project the cool dignity the occasion demanded instead of the childish insecurity she was feeling inside.

The main cause of her inner quaking hadn't arrived yet, she saw. Relieved, she sought out her grandfather and headed toward him.

Fortunate enough to catch him in a rare moment alone, Tracy briefly squeezed his hand. "Does the polished company brass seem a bit tarnished, Mac?" she asked in a low voice. "The camaraderie around here a trifle forced?"

"I certainly stirred up a tempest with my casual remark about retiring, didn't I?" Mac admitted.

"You certainly did. That *supposedly* casual comment of yours gave the business columnists a field day and definitely unsheathed the knives of your would-be successors." Tracy suppressed a grin. "You did it on purpose, didn't you," she said. "A month ago you got bored, so you dropped that so-called inadvertent comment into the midst of those hungry executives and journalists the way you tossed a cherry bomb into the center of a gang of schoolyard bullies when you were a kid. You just wanted to watch the excitement, right? Maybe see whether Sunstone's stock would waver?"

"And it's solid," Mac said proudly. "It's a fine company, strong enough to get along whether I'm heading it or not."

"Don't you even *think* that way!" Tracy said, her voice still low but fierce. "Sunstone needs you. It'll need you for a long time to come."

"I'm seventy-five, princess," he gently reminded her.

"Princess?" she repeated, her brow furrowed in mock severity. She and Mac were careful to keep their relationship formal in public, especially around their business associates. As one of several Sunstone executives, Tracy preferred not to flaunt her special closeness to the chairman of the board.

"Sorry," Mac said, not looking sorry at all. "I forgot our rule for a minute. But you do look like a princess tonight. I like your dress. That light blue color suits you," Mac said as he glanced toward the ballroom's entrance and nodded approvingly. "Good. Nick has arrived."

Tracy's heart skipped a beat and her fingers dug into her palms as she battled the sudden onslaught of emotions Mac's words aroused. Her brief respite had ended. Nick Corcoran had arrived.

She made herself follow Mac's gaze, hoping a miracle had unexpectedly cured her of Corcoranitis. But no, the usual symptoms struck the instant she saw him—constricted throat, labored breathing, blanked-out brain.

No matter how many times and ways she tried to talk herself out of her infatuation with Nick, her body betrayed her whenever he was near, and she couldn't seem to get over her malady.

The trouble was, she was suffering from a simple crush on an unattainable, good-looking man. Yes, her pulse raced and hot tingles of excitement rippled over her when she looked at him, and, yes, it was partly because he was gorgeous. With his rough-hewn features and lean but athletic build, Nick shouldn't look good in black tie, she thought, yet he carried off his evening clothes with the casual elegance he brought to everything he did.

Tracy could have handled a simple matter of physical attraction. Unfortunately what she felt for Nick was so much more. She *liked* him. And admired him. And trusted him. But she was painfully aware that those feelings were not mutual. Nick didn't like, admire, or trust Tracy Carlisle.

He was alone, she noted with undeniable satisfaction. No striking brunette with a jungle-goddess name like Tanya was draped over his arm. She saw no sexy redhead called Mirielle with a Parisian accent and generous, pouty lips. It would be a relief not to have to pretend to welcome one of his lady friends.

Mac's voice jarred her from her private thoughts. "Tracy, would you greet Nick and make sure he gets a drink?"

Tracy's stomach twisted into knots. She was

tempted to bolt. Why couldn't Mac greet his second-in-command himself, she wondered frantically.

But she wouldn't panic, she simply wouldn't. "Of course," she murmured. On the way to her untimely fate she instructed a waiter to get a scotch on the rocks for Nick, and a moment later she was thrusting out her hand to him as eagerly as if she were sticking it into an open flame. "Good evening, Nick," she said in a tiny voice that was the best she could manage. "Glad you could make it." Inwardly she groaned. What a stupid thing to say! The dinner party was an annual company event, the kickoff to a week-long retreat at Sunstone Lodge. All the company executives were flying to the lodge the next morning. Naturally Nick had made it. "You must be glad to leave New York's heat wave behind," she went on, hating herself for resorting to the weather as a topic for conversation. But her mind wouldn't operate and she was suffering her own heat wave. She also was half intoxicated by the delicious scent of Nick's aftershave. How could she be expected to have full use of her faculties? Besides, aware that her maddening shyness appeared to be haughtiness— her sister Alison had told her she had to be more outgoing or she'd seem like a dreadful snob—she froze all the more, knowing the impression she was giving. Still she had to try, she realized. "At least there's a cool breeze in the Windy City," she mumbled.

Nick had leaned forward slightly to catch what she was saying and frowned, caught off guard by an elusive scent of flowers that reminded him of wild meadows in summer. Something was wrong, he decided. The fragrance didn't suit Tracy Carlisle. She wasn't the wild-meadow type. She was pretty, yes. In fact, he had to admit she was a beauty with her nicely-shaped figure, her porcelainlike skin, her honey-blond hair, and her wide-set, enormous sapphire eyes.

But wild meadows? No. Tracy was more like a tiny, perfect ornament, a bit of crystal, multifaceted and reflecting diffused light like the twinkling pear-shaped drops that hung from the chandeliers overhead.

When the waiter brought his scotch on the rocks—his favorite brand—Nick was impressed. There was nothing wrong with Tracy's memory—or her skills as Mac's hostess.

All right, Nick thought impatiently, silently arguing with himself. Tracy was a competent woman. Fine. She even was interesting in a way. He had to concede that much. More than once he'd caught himself musing about what might be hidden within her icy depths. But it certainly couldn't be desire he felt for her, he told himself. He wasn't about to hurt or enhance his future at Sunstone by getting tangled up with her.

Suddenly he returned his attention to Tracy's words. What had she said? Something about the weather? "With air-conditioned offices and cars and apartments," he muttered without a smile, "even an August heat wave in New York isn't hard to take." Without air-conditioning, he remembered too vividly, a New York heat wave could be sheer hell. He lifted his glass of scotch and took a healthy swig, refusing to think about those days. "I suppose you'll be going up to the lake tomorrow along with the rest of us," he remarked a moment later, uncomfortable about his near rudeness toward Tracy. For some reason she affected him as no one else could.

Tracy nodded. "It should be nice up there at this time of year if the weather holds." Oh, no, she thought, wishing she could wrinkle her nose like a television witch and disappear. She'd mentioned the weather again? "But August is usually lovely," she heard herself ramble on.

Nick raised his scotch to his lips again as it occurred to him that a week in the Canadian wilderness with a bunch of men—and Beryl Judson, the only other woman—couldn't be a pleasant prospect for a cosseted girl like Tracy. She was accustomed to the luxury of Mac's home, a restored nineteenth-century mansion. Mac's lodge in the forest was comfortable but simple, even rustic. "Those sessions must be a bit of a trial for you. How do you survive them?" he asked in a rare burst of sympathy for a young woman who had to try to live up to the image of a man like Bill MacKay and compete with a band of corporate jackals . . . himself included.

Tracy privately agreed that spending a week in Nick's company was a severe trial, but she wasn't about to say so. Even without the emotional distress of being with Nick day and night while enduring his indifference, she found little enjoyment in being surrounded by a dozen men who pretended to appreciate the isolated northern lake in order to impress Mac. There was also the aggravation of having to ward off some none-too-subtle flirting from colleagues who saw her as a shortcut to Mac's good graces and tried to use the isolation of the forest lodge to get close to her. She felt vulnerable, as she was the only woman they picked on that way. Beryl Judson, head of the company's international public relations firm, didn't seem to arouse the same reactions, but that wasn't surprising to Tracy. Beryl was more macho than most of the men, and they weren't inclined to make passes at her.

Tracy liked Beryl, who had worked at Sunstone for nearly three decades and wasn't easily impressed or cowed by anyone. Whenever Beryl was being particularly blunt—including to the chairman himself—Tracy smiled to herself as she'd peek at the shocked faces of the corporate climbers who couldn't seem to grasp the fact that Mac thoroughly enjoyed the exchanges.

She had another reason to like Nick Corcoran, Tracy reflected. He enjoyed those exchanges, too, his admiration for the crusty Beryl obvious. He wasn't afraid to back her in a discussion with Mac if he thought she was right. But, then, Nick understood that Bill MacKay appreciated honesty in an employee and despised toadying yes-men.

As she glanced at her grandfather, Tracy's heart swelled with pride. The man was magnificent: handsome, charming, tall, and broad-shouldered. Mac exuded strength and virility. His thick white hair, always perfectly cut and groomed, framed a tanned face that boasted the wickedest grin and most devilishly twinkling azure eyes Tracy had ever seen.

No man could ever fill Mac's shoes, Tracy thought, then slowly turned her attention back to Nick, amending her opinion slightly.

Perhaps one man could.

Looking at Nick left her struggling to breathe, she remembered too late. His eyes drew hers with an irresistible magnetism, and his mouth was a dangerous temptation she could barely resist, a hard yet sensual mouth that made her own lips tingle when she mentally traced its contours. How often had she imagined it brushing over her skin or nibbling at her swollen lower lip, possessively teasing what she eagerly offered . . . ?

Possessively? she thought with a silent laugh. What a dreamer she was.

It was hard to pretend detachment when she ached to tousle Nick's silky chestnut hair, when each time she saw him she wished she had the freedom or the nerve to stare blatantly at him long enough to memorize his slightly bumpy nose, his chiseled jawline, his determined chin. Even his fingers riveted her. Long and tapered, they looked strong yet sensitive enough to create sweet sensations in a woman.

Remembering where and who she was, Tracy took a deep breath and clenched her jaw, trying to get herself under control before she did something outrageous like throw her arms around him and whisper "Take me, you fool."

Nick saw her almost imperceptible gesture and wished he could read minds. He'd asked her a question about the trips to the lodge; she'd simply chosen to ignore it. Accustomed to capturing and holding women's attention, Nick was always taken aback by Tracy's cool disdain. She didn't care for his question so she didn't answer it. She simply looked calmly around the room as if he'd ceased to exist. Against his will he was intrigued by Tracy. What had she been thinking when she'd turned to stare at Mac? What was going through her mind? Was she sizing up the competition? Wondering how to turn her grandfather against any upstarts who might get in the way of her ambitions? She had the advantage: Mac clearly adored her. She, however, never showed an ounce of affection for the old man—not in public, at any rate.

Tracy realized that she and Nick had begun staring mutely at each other. Then she noticed that Nick's glass was empty. She managed a bright smile. "If you'll excuse me, I'll find someone to refresh your drink." Not a brilliant choice of words, she told herself as she moved toward a waiter, but at least she hadn't given Nick another up-to-the-minute meteorological report.

After she'd ordered another scotch for him, she moved through the small groups of guests, stopping here and there to chat. Tracy worked the crowd, appearing to enjoy the social-butterfly role when in truth she hated it. Glancing across the room, she smiled at Beryl Judson as the woman caught her grandfather's arm.

"Beryl," Mac said, planting a kiss on her cheek. "Just the person I need to be with."

"Fun and games, huh?" she said in her throaty voice, her weathered face creased in a frown. She moved closer to Mac and tilted her head back as if to aim her confidential words directly into his ear.

"So who's your choice to succeed you when you do retire, say ten years from now?" Beryl asked with her usual bluntness.

"Who's yours?" Mac returned.

"No contest. Nick. And he's yours as well. That's why you wooed him into the Sunstone fold three years ago. The boy's a rarity; he's not too caught up in his own self-importance to see what needs to be done." Beryl's pursed lips suddenly curved in a grin. "And not that it makes any difference, but he's a good-looking devil. Like you. He'll be easy to market to the press and the public. Even that angry-young-man aura about him is appealing. He's your paladin, Bill. A chivalrous crusader in the cause of what's right for Sunstone."

"And for Nick Corcoran," Mac added realistically.

Beryl snorted. "Of course for Nick Corcoran. I said he was chivalrous. I didn't say he was an idiot." She took a sip of her champagne, then indicated Tracy with an inclination of her head. "Why haven't we considered your granddaughter? Is she too young?"

"Can you keep a secret?" Mac asked.

Beryl nodded.

"Tracy doesn't want my job," he said honestly.

"She refuses to admit you're ever going to retire, does she?"

"It's partly that, but she's like us. She thinks Nick is the right person to take my place."

"She thinks Nick is the right person for everything," Beryl said with a smile.

Mac grinned at the woman. "You don't miss much, do you? Or is Tracy wearing her heart on her sleeve? I thought I knew what the girl was feeling because she and I are so close. She certainly hasn't talked to me about it."

"Bill, Tracy's always been your little buddy, trailing after you to the office even as a child, so I've known her since she was a toddler. I can read the girl pretty well. She's not wearing her heart on her sleeve. In fact, when she's around Nick Corcoran she freezes up so solid I'd swear she doesn't have a heart at all. That was my first clue. My second was the way she keeps sneaking peeks at him when he's not looking. Adoration fairly glows from those great blue eyes of hers."

"I know," Mac said.

"But do you know," Beryl said with a wise gleam in her eyes, "that Nick does the same thing? Stand back sometime—tonight, for instance—and watch where his gaze invariably goes. Then watch how he tenses up, maybe tosses back a swig of scotch, bee-lines for some other attractive woman, and within minutes is seeking Tracy out again. Just watch, Bill. And put on your thinking cap for a change."

"For a change?" he repeated, laughing. "I concede I haven't noticed as much as you, but I'm aware that Nick is more attracted to Tracy than he admits or even realizes."

"Then why haven't you done anything about it?" Beryl demanded. "All those two kids need is a chance to be alone for a while, long enough so Tracy's self-control cracks a little and Nick sees that there's a real live person in there. Can't you arrange something, Bill?"

"I don't like to interfere."

Beryl gave a little snort of disgust. "You didn't mind interfering back when you wanted Margaret and she was engaged to somebody else, did you? And were you ever sorry? Not for a moment. Look at this situation in the light of what's best for Sunstone. Did you slog through forests staking claims and prospecting all those years, did you plant yourself in bankers' offices until they financed your company just to get rid of you, did you work like a fool so you could turn this corporation over to the likes of Hugh Harlan? Nick Corcoran *has* to be your replacement when the time comes for you to smell the wildflowers. He wants the job. Tracy doesn't. Tracy wants Nick. Nick wants Tracy, whether he knows it or not. And you say you won't interfere? Come on, Bill. Get with it."

Laughing heartily by this time, Mac put his arm around Beryl's shoulder and gave her a quick hug. "So what do I do?" he asked.

Beryl grinned at him. "Now, Bill, you were smart enough to build a huge international conglomerate. Surely you can think of a way to give your granddaughter a chance to have her heart's desire and take care of Sunstone's future at the same time. Or have I overestimated you all these years?"

Mac stared at his old friend for several moments. "You know, I believe I *can* come up with something," he said at last. Glancing at Nick as the young man stared daggers at David Henderson, who was giving Tracy his undivided attention, Mac nodded. "And it seems it's time I did." Raising his glass and waiting for Beryl to do the same, he winked conspiratorially at her. "Here's to good old-fashioned matchmaking, Beryl. Let's hope it works."

Two

The week of retreat at Sunstone Lodge was finally drawing to a close with a speech by Hugh Harlan that made it embarrassingly obvious he was trying to present himself as Mac's natural successor.

Tracy listened with forced patience, trying not to drum her fingertips on the wooden arm of her chair or tap her toe on the pine-planked floor.

Of all the company retreats she'd spent at Sunstone Lodge, this had been the worst. The backstabbing she'd watched for the past week had been eye-opening and disillusioning. But the retreat *was* over, she reminded herself, or would be if Hugh ever stopped talking. With a glance at Beryl to see how she was reacting to Hugh's droning, Tracy nearly laughed aloud. Beryl was asleep.

Smart woman, Tracy thought, beginning to cringe as Hugh stabbed the air dramatically to underscore his awful clichés. Hugh's father had been such a special man, it bothered Tracy not to be able to respect his son. She tried, but Hugh wasn't the least bit like his dad, or even competent in his own way. Hugh was his mother's son. Her puppet. Louise Harlan, a regular Lady Macbeth, had probably written his speech, chiding him about how he had to be prepared to take the Sunstone helm when Mac stepped down.

Mac would *never* step down, Tracy told herself fiercely. Certainly not for a very long time. He was too vibrant.

As always when she allowed herself to think about Mac's eventual successor, her gaze crept to Nick Corcoran.

What a week it had been for her, so close to Nick day and night with nothing to show for it but increased frustration. The man simply couldn't stand her. Why couldn't she just accept that fact and forget about him?

The trouble was, her admiration for Nick seemed boundless, especially now that so many of the other executives were displaying a marked lack of grace under pressure and Nick refused to sink to their level. He was wonderful, and such a fair man too. He'd defended her when she'd been criticized by Hugh and some of the others for her stance on the question of expansion. Hugh insisted she was hurting the whole of Sunstone by deliberately curbing her own division's growth. Nick hadn't agreed. "I'm with Tracy," he'd said. What a lovely phrase, Tracy thought as she replayed it over and over in her mind, recalling how she'd almost lapsed into an adoring trance when she'd first heard those words.

Nick had been her only ally. Mac had been acting as moderator and refraining from getting involved in any discussions. "I'm definitely with Tracy on this," Nick had repeated, warming her heart and stiffening her backbone. She knew she was right, but it was a comfort to have such formidable support —and a joy that it was Nick who was providing it.

Tracy's video production company, along with her chain of rental outlets, was her own brainchild, and like a parent, she felt she understood what was best for her five-year-old youngster. So did Nick. "The whole video operation was Tracy's idea," he'd pointed out. "Her business plan, her marketing scheme. Carlisle Videos' quarterly statements have shown phenomenal growth from day one . . . you might even say abnormal growth. But, as Tracy has noted, the market shows signs of leveling out, and I say she's right to hold the line on further expansion for now. It's up to her to decide when the time is right to move ahead and when it's better to stand pat." Piercing each dissenting executive in turn with his penetrating gaze, Nick had paused, then added his zinger. "Anyone here whose division can top or even equal the bottom-line figures of Carlisle Videos can justifiably question Tracy's management decisions. Otherwise . . ."

Nick hadn't needed to finish his sentence. Carlisle Videos had been the unquestioned leader of all the Sunstone divisions for several quarters, and everyone knew it. Tracy told herself there was nothing personal in Nick's support, but two days later her heart was still singing.

Realizing she'd been daydreaming, she forced herself to pay attention to Hugh again, though she was amazed he was still talking. She noticed he was preaching expansion in every division despite the fact that at the end of the free discussions Mac had come out firmly against it.

Interesting, Tracy thought. Hugh challenging Mac? That had never happened before.

She heard the hum of a motor as a small Cessna landed on the lake, the first of several float planes that would take the Sunstone people back to town. The shareholders' meeting was a few days away, allowing time for the group to check in with families and branch offices before returning to Chicago.

The scene outside the room's huge picture window lured Tracy's attention from Hugh again as she watched a playful breeze gently set the birch, oak, and maple leaves to dancing. She wished she could stay with Mac after everyone else had gone. She sighed softly. She couldn't stay. Mac had asked her to go back to Chicago right away to oversee preparations for the shareholders' meeting while he remained at the lake for another couple of days. Though she worried about him being alone in the lodge—there wasn't even a telephone in the place—she couldn't blame him for craving the solitude and peace of the woods. So, as always, she obeyed Mac unhesitatingly.

Back to reality, she reminded herself again. Hugh was showing no signs of reaching the end of his speech. Finally, when all the float planes had landed on the lake, Mac's quietly compelling voice suggested that Hugh wind up his remarks.

Clearly annoyed, Hugh glared at the chairman, then deliberately carried on with his talk.

Tracy was shocked. What was this, an open rebellion? Had the mere suggestion that Mac might retire made Hugh think his presidency would automatically lead to the chairmanship? Had Louise persuaded her son he was on the verge of being in command?

Beryl saved the day by waking up and moving for adjournment at a moment when Hugh paused to look down at his notes. Someone seconded the motion, and Hugh had to concede defeat.

In a flash Nick was on his feet and bearing down on Tracy, his long legs covering the distance between them in three strides. She gaped at him, trying not to dwell on how wonderful he looked in the fawn-colored cotton slacks and beige polo shirt that showed his tanned, muscular body to breathtaking advantage. "I'll meet you at the dock," he said abruptly, looking for all the world as if he intended to drown her once he got her there. Turning on his heel, he started out of the room but paused to talk briefly with two of the other men, his tone and manner with them perfectly civil.

Tracy blinked several times. Meet Nick at the dock? Why? So he could tie boulders to her ankles and toss her into the drink?

She felt a gentle touch on her shoulder and turned to find Mac smiling down at her. "Come to the upstairs sitting room, will you?" he asked in a low voice.

Tracy nodded, took a quick peek at Nick's lithe form, then followed her grandfather up the spiral staircase that joined the upper and lower levels of the lodge.

The view from the upper room broadened the panorama Tracy had been admiring downstairs, and for a moment she forgot her confusion.

She could see the dock where the first float plane was already collecting its passengers, foolish men hurrying to escape the forest and return to the more familiar urban jungle. A week of getting back to nature hadn't taught them a thing, Tracy mused.

Mac went to the far end of the room, opened a pine cupboard, removed a small object, and took it to Tracy. ·

She wasn't surprised to see that he was presenting her with a rock about the size of a tennis ball. "How's this for a pudding-stone specimen?" he asked proudly. "Add it to your collection."

Tracy grinned with a rush of affection. She'd started gathering rocks years earlier for a school project when Mac, as a geologist and prospector, could help her. She'd gotten top marks, and somehow the collection had just kept growing. "Where did you find this?" she asked, turning the colorful stone over and over in the palm of her hand.

"I was visiting an old geologist buddy of mine at his cottage on that little lake where I used to fish, and this bit of pudding stone was lying right on shore."

"You polished it," Tracy murmured, pleased. The gift might have meant little to someone else, but to her it brought back sweet memories of times she and Mac had shared. With a kiss to his cheek, she whispered, "Thank you."

Mac laughed. "You know, it occurs to me that most men probably give their lovely granddaughters different kinds of rocks. Rubies and emeralds, for instance."

"They're short on imagination," Tracy said. "I'll take pudding stone any day."

"I always knew you had good taste," Mac said, giving her a hug. "And now you'd better get a move on." He glanced out the window. "Nick's already down at the dock waiting for you."

Tracy's head snapped up and she followed Mac's gaze. "Why?"

"Didn't I mention it? I asked Nick to give you a hand in Chicago, so you two will have to travel together."

Tracy swallowed hard, then spoke carefully. "Nick and I? In the little Cessna? Then in the company plane for the trip back to Chicago? Just the two of us?"

"Is that a problem?" Mac asked with feigned innocence.

Tracy stared at him, dumbfounded. Was it a problem? No. Just a disaster. To be alone with Nick was a dream. To be alone with him and enduring his obvious annoyance at being stuck with her was a nightmare.

She turned away from Mac and went over to his bookshelf, determined to hide her dismay. "No," she said in a small voice. "It's not a problem. May I borrow something to read on the trip?" She grabbed a Charles Dickens anthology, planning to lose herself in the guillotine scenes of *A Tale of Two Cities* or something equally cheerful, managed a bright smile for Mac, and headed for the stairway. "I'd better go to my room and get my things," she said, proud that she wasn't betraying the tumult of emotions making her heart thud wildly and her legs go rubbery.

"I'll see you downstairs, then," Mac said pleasantly.

She hesitated on the second step, suddenly troubled by an anxiety she couldn't pinpoint, something that went beyond her nervousness about traveling with Nick. "Do you absolutely insist on staying here alone?" she asked.

Mac rolled his eyes. "You're such a worry-wart. I've stayed alone in this country in far less comfortable circumstances than this since your grandmother died." He grinned. "I'll be fine."

Tracy knew she would spoil Mac's enjoyment of his little holiday by nagging him, so she forced a smile. Then, still plagued by a fleeting sensation of dread, she ran back, threw her arms around her grandfather, and hugged him with all her might. "I love you," she whispered. "Be careful, okay?"

Mac wrapped his arms around Tracy. "Get a move on, honey," he said huskily. "I want you out of here before the storm moves in. Don't you still have to go to your room to get your bag?"

"I don't have much and I'm all packed," she replied in a small voice, reluctantly deciding she had to go. "Will you be down at the dock to say good-bye?"

"I'll wave from the front door," Mac said. He winked at her. "There's enough confusion on the dock now with all those city boys fighting to be the first to leave the wilderness."

Tracy grinned and headed for the stairway.

"By the way . . ." Mac said.

She looked back at him, her brow raised questioningly.

"I love you too," he told her.

She nodded, then hurried away before her nagging fears made her blubber like a child.

Nick paced the dock, impatiently waiting for Tracy. Where was she anyway, he wondered absently as he thought over what Mac had asked him to do. Why did Tracy need his help to oversee the preparations for the shareholders' meeting? Was Mac expecting some kind of trouble he was afraid Tracy couldn't handle alone? It didn't make sense: Nick couldn't picture any situation Tracy Carlisle would be unable to handle.

Still, he thought, Mac always had his reasons, and if he wanted Tracy to have backup in Chicago, so be it.

Nick didn't look forward to the trip, however. They had nothing to say to each other and even the brief silences between them were awkward. And as hard as he'd tried not to notice Tracy over the past few days, he hadn't succeeded. His gaze had focused on her no matter who was with her or where they'd been. Never before had a woman so captivated his attention, especially not in a business setting. Where Sunstone was concerned, Nick was all business, but all he had to do was look at Tracy and very unbusiness-like things came to mind. His only consolation was knowing that she wasn't the least bit interested in him.

Where the hell *was* she? He stopped pacing and stood on the dock facing the lodge, feet apart, hands resting loosely on his hips.

Finally he saw Tracy emerge from the house, pause to shake hands with her grandfather, then head down the path to the lake.

She was so little, Nick found himself thinking. In her sneakers and jeans and an oversize blue T-shirt she struck him as even more fragile than in her business or evening clothes. And she'd worn her hair in a ponytail all week, which was so out of character for her, Nick had done several double takes. "All set?" he asked gruffly, resisting an insane urge to pick her up and deposit her in the plane as if she were a helpless child.

She nodded, saying nothing, her eyes downcast.

Nick reached for her nylon duffel bag. "This is it?" he asked, surprised.

Tracy nodded again but didn't release the bag. "I can manage," she said quietly.

"Okay," he said, shrugging. "I guess we can go, then."

As she reached the plane, she stepped onto the pontoons and hoisted her bag and then herself inside the cabin before Nick had a chance to play the gentleman and help her.

Independent little thing, he mused, settling beside her as she stowed the bag under her seat.

Suddenly, looking at the pilot, she froze, then spoke in a wary, clipped tone. "Where's Frank Duggan?"

The pilot turned to smile at his passengers. "Frank took sick, I'm afraid. He thinks it's the flu. You don't need to worry, I'm not a colorful old bush pilot like Frank, but I'm competent. The name's Walt Cooper. By the way, Frank said to tell you he's sorry."

Nick could see that Tracy had taken an instant dislike to the man, and he wasn't sure why. Cooper was neatly dressed, seemed polite enough.

Tracy pressed her lips together as if forcing herself to accept the substitution with good grace, looked out the window, and waved to Mac.

"Seat belt done up?" Nick asked, checking even after she'd given him her usual nod. He was suddenly gripped by a surge of protectiveness. Tracy's expression was almost forlorn, and, dammit, she did seem so tiny and delicate. Any red-blooded male would have passing moments of protectiveness toward her, he told himself.

It occurred to Nick that Tracy might be afraid of flying, especially in a small plane instead of the luxurious company aircraft or the Concordes and jumbo jets she was used to. "Nervous?" he asked in a low voice, trying to smile at her.

Her china-blue eyes widened for an instant before she gathered her composure again. "Of flying?" she asked guardedly.

It was Nick's turn to nod.

Tracy looked out the window again as she answered. "I like flying," she murmured.

He wasn't sure she'd fully answered his question, but it was obvious she was very edgy about something. Did small changes in plans upset her? If so, wasn't that a weakness her business rivals would have exploited? Then why, Nick asked himself, did he have to keep battling the urge to put his arm around her slim shoulders and reassure her that everything was going to be all right?

The pilot taxied the Cessna out onto the open lake and moments later they were airborne.

When Sunstone Lake was finally out of sight, she reached under the seat for her bag, took out a thick book, and opened it.

Taking a peek at what Tracy was reading, Nick wondered at her utter lack of humor. The book was open at one of the most amusing passages of *Pickwick Papers*, yet she wasn't so much as cracking a smile.

He understood why after another five minutes when she hadn't turned a single page.

Tracy was staring at the book but she wasn't reading.

"You like Dickens?" he asked impulsively.

She dragged her gaze from the page and stared blankly at him for several long seconds before replying. "Very much," she said at last.

Two words, Nick thought. He'd managed to get two whole words out of the lady. The old Corcoran charm was as irresistible as ever.

Then Tracy began looking at her watch. She established a rhythm: glance out the window, crane her neck a little to study the landscape below, gaze into the wild blue yonder, stare at her watch, and scowl.

"My favorite Dickens novel will always be *A Christmas Carol*," Nick heard himself saying. No one could claim he wasn't persistent, he thought.

Tracy made a poor attempt at a smile. "*Great Expectations* is mine."

It would be, Nick thought sardonically. He'd never known anyone—not personally, anyway—born with greater expectations than Tracy Carlisle.

He abandoned his efforts at conversation and let her pretend to read. He was fascinated by the tense way she kept checking the terrain and looking at her watch.

Suddenly she leaned close to him and spoke barely above a whisper. "Something's wrong."

At that moment the plane's engine sputtered, and Nick's whole body went tight, coiling for action. Half unaware of what he was doing, he reached for Tracy's hand and held it, belatedly realizing his first impulse had been to comfort her.

But she didn't need his comfort. After an initial startled glance at the pilot, she showed no further emotion and merely chewed delicately on her lower lip while using her free hand to tuck her book back into her duffel bag.

"Don't worry, folks," the pilot called back to them. "We're having some kind of engine trouble, but we're right over a lake, so I'll just set this baby down and have a look."

Nick glanced at Tracy and smiled. Her expression remained grave and she slowly shook her head, her eyes narrowed, her brain clearly operating at full tilt. Nick almost could see her thinking, but he had no idea what was going through her mind.

Walt Cooper had been right, Nick decided minutes later. The man was competent. He'd put the plane down smoothly, then started taxiing toward shore. "So, no big deal, right?" Nick said to Tracy, disturbed by her continued tension. "A little delay isn't much to worry about in the grand scheme of things."

Tracy's knuckles were white as she gripped her bag and leaned toward him again. "I don't suppose you have any kind of weapon," she whispered.

Nick gaped at her. Tracy wasn't the hysterical type. Why would she ask if he had a weapon? He shook his head. "Not even a Swiss army knife," he admitted as the plane came to a complete stop.

Tracy hesitated, then reached into her bag and pulled out a battered old jackknife and started to hand it to him.

"Just put it down, little girl," the pilot said.

Nick turned his head to stare at Walt Cooper. He found himself looking into the ugly black muzzle of a gun.

Three

Tracy let the knife drop to the floor, then flinched as Nick curved his arm around her shoulders and slanted his body to shield her from Walt's gun. Insanely her heart pounded with a thrill and joy that really didn't fit the circumstances. Staring at Nick, she wondered whether he'd think her terribly forward if she crawled over onto his lap.

She gave herself a mental shake. They were in serious trouble!

"Now, you two just climb out of the plane, slow and easy," Cooper was saying.

Deciding not to argue with the pilot's .44 Magnum, Nick went first, then turned to lift Tracy down to the decrepit dock, all the while cursing himself for being a fool. Obviously Tracy had sensed danger from the start, but he'd been blithely unconcerned, the perfect victim. Some troubleshooter he was.

But there was no sense wasting time blaming himself. He had to figure a way out of this mess.

For once he was grateful for Tracy's cool self-control. She even managed to smile at him as he set her down on the dock. Her quiet courage touched him, and he kept his arm around her waist, determined to shield her from harm at any cost—for Mac's sake, of course, he told himself. Mac wouldn't be able to bear it if anything happened to his granddaughter.

It came as no surprise that another armed man was waiting on the dock, impatiently motioning Nick and Tracy toward him. "That's Red," Cooper informed them as he got out of the plane. "Follow him and don't try anything. I'm right behind you."

"Who's the guy?" Red asked when the others reached him. "I thought we were only after the girl."

"That's what I thought too," Cooper answered. "But there was a last-minute change in the arrangements, so we got two for one. Don't worry. The word is that the old man has a soft spot for Corcoran here, too, so having him just strengthens our hand."

Both Nick and Tracy remained silent, neither of them bothering to state the obvious: they were the latest victims in a recent rash of executive kidnappings.

Nick had to release Tracy so they could walk single file along the narrow dock. She felt bereft but told herself she could think more clearly undistracted by the warmth of his touch.

Her dominating emotion was disgust that she and Nick had fallen into the trap. It especially bugged her that she'd chosen to remain silent at the beginning of the trip despite her immediate suspicions. Besotted with Nick and nervous at the prospect of traveling with him, she'd let down her guard so badly, she hadn't even thought to get Mac down to the plane to check Cooper out. Dumb. Really dumb, she berated herself.

One of the boards under her feet gave way but she managed not to trip. A sprained ankle was the last thing she needed now. "This dock needs repairs," she commented. "It's rickety." As so often happened when she was frightened, upset, angry, or all three as she was now, she resorted to her own brand of black humor. "These old docks should stand up better," she muttered, glancing back over her shoulder at Nick. "They're made of hickory."

He said nothing, thinking it was an odd time for Tracy to choose for a chat.

She took another step, checked to be sure the boards ahead were solid, then looked back at Nick again, her mouth quirking in a tiny grin. "Which makes this a rickety hickory dock, right?"

He stared at her with a pained expression that suggested he was afraid her mind had snapped.

Tracy wondered the same thing. But she was only whistling in the dark, trying to reassure Nick she wasn't about to cave in. She was also falling back on her grandfather's lessons about dealing with intimidating people. "Never let them know you're afraid," Mac had taught her. "Act as if you're scared of nothing and you might even believe it yourself."

"Move it, funny girl," Walt ordered.

Tracy made a face at him just to let him know she was undaunted, then continued to follow Red, who led the way toward a tiny ramshackle cabin not far from the lakeshore. She noticed that every once in a while the carrot-topped scarecrow of a man looked back at her with a decided leer.

Nick's mind was reeling. Where had this cheeky little Tracy Carlisle come from? Who was she? This gutsy lady certainly bore no resemblance to the soft-spoken gentlewoman he remembered as Mac's grand-daughter.

And while he was wondering about identities, who was this Nick Corcoran whose insides clenched with fury every time Red subjected Tracy to his bold scrutiny? Nick Corcoran didn't care a fig for Tracy Carlisle, so why did he want to smash his fist into Red's unshaven face every time the man so much as glanced her way?

Tracy was more practical. Red was a singularly unappealing fellow, but if he thought himself a ladies' man, she would find a way to use his silly conceit against him. "Look for weaknesses," she could almost hear Mac instructing her. "Check for vulnerabilities and make use of them."

Suddenly Red tripped over a jagged rock and walked into a nest of burdocks that attached themselves to his pantlegs. At the same time, he struck out with his free hand at a buzzing mosquito, muttering curses.

Great, Tracy thought triumphantly. Red was out of his element in the northern bush. Now, that was a little weakness she really might be able to take advantage of.

All at once an unpleasant thought hit her. "What's the true story on Frank Duggan? I'd hate to be you if you've hurt Frank in any way. My grandfather wouldn't like that."

"Gol-ly," Walt said. "Can't you just see me shaking in my boots?"

"You should be," Tracy said, glaring at him. She was only half bluffing. If Walt Cooper didn't realize the caliber of opponent he'd chosen in going up against Bill MacKay, he was a stupid man.

"Inside," Walt said as they reached the cabin.

The place was filthy, Tracy saw at once. Cobwebs laced every corner, the droppings of mice and larger creatures sprinkled the floor, and chunks had been chewed out of the ancient wooden table pushed against one wall. Two iron-frame beds in the middle of the single room were covered by dirty mattresses torn in several places and undoubtedly housing nests of fieldmice.

"Charming," Tracy muttered with calculated disdain. She knew her reputation as Mac's spoiled little girl. Perhaps it would come in handy now. Slowly circling the room with the most regal, haughty attitude she could summon, she checked out the contents: a brand new sleeping bag still rolled in its carrying sack and bearing its price tag; two boy scout cooking kits on the wood stove; envelopes of dried food obviously purchased on the advice of some survivalist-store clerk who knew an easy mark when he saw one; an ax leaning against the stove. An ax. Was there a chance that Red and Walt would be careless . . . ? She pretended not to notice the weapon. "My goodness," she said, her voice dripping with sarcasm. "I should have thought even kidnappers lived like civilized creatures. This is really quite dreadful, gentlemen."

"What's the going rate for corporate executives?" Nick asked Cooper in the hope of distracting the man's attention from Tracy.

"That's not on your need-to-know list," Walt answered, but didn't take his eyes off Tracy for a second. "So this little home away from home isn't good enough for you, lady?"

She smiled sweetly. "It isn't even good enough for

a couple of low-life thugs like you, Mr. Cooper. I trust you'll order your lackey here to do some cleaning?"

Red scowled. "Hey, what did she call me? Who's she think she is anyway?"

"Your ticket to fortune," she answered. "Unless, of course, my grandfather refuses to pay up—which is entirely possible. He doesn't believe in giving in to hoodlums."

"He will, little girl," Walt said smoothly. "He'll do exactly what he's told." Walt picked up a coil of rope and tossed it to Red. "Tie Corcoran to that chair in the corner. He looks like he's just itching to make trouble."

Nick wanted to fight Red but didn't dare. Alone he might have had a chance against these men, but he had to play along or endanger Tracy. He let Red push him into the chair and wind the rope around him, wondering how badly he'd regret his passiveness.

Tracy wasn't surprised that Nick was being tied up. She just hoped Walt didn't have the same plans for her. But maybe she could ensure her freedom. It was worth a try. "So which of you charming fellows will be cooking up these gourmet-meals-in-an-envelope?" she asked with more than a hint of mockery in her voice.

"Well, now, I thought that would be a good job for you, little girl," Walt told her. "After you clean up the joint, that is."

"I'm not a servant," she said.

Walt tipped back his head and laughed, then abruptly changed his mood and leveled a cold gaze at her. "You're a servant if I say so, and I do say so. You want this place cleaned up? Start cleaning. Then you can fix a nice meal for the three of you while I go back to that fancy lodge and talk to Grandpa."

Casually he walked over to the stove and picked up the ax, testing the blade as he looked at Nick. "What I need is some proof that I've got you two. A couple of fingers ought to do it."

Tracy's coolness left her. The blood drained from her face, and her stomach turned over. She couldn't move as she watched Walt move purposefully toward Nick.

"Free his hand for a minute," Walt told Red. "Then hold his wrist."

Nick had never experienced such helplessness, and he couldn't accept what was about to happen. He stared fixedly at Walt, watching as the pilot raised the ax and took aim. The blade descended. Nick braced himself for the pain.

Suddenly Tracy screamed and threw herself against Walt, surprising him with enough sheer force to knock the ax out of his grip and send it clattering across the table and onto the floor.

Walt wheeled around, his eyes blazing as he advanced on her. Nick battled in vain to free himself.

Tracy saw Walt's fury and decided her only defense was to fly into a tantrum of her own. It wasn't difficult. Not after what the man had intended to do to Nick. "You idiot!" she shouted, grabbing one of the boy scout kits and heaving it so it whizzed past Walt's head. "You blundering know-nothing! Haven't you done any homework at all? Don't you realize what you almost did just now?"

"Tracy," Nick said, grateful to her but sickened by the thought that all she was doing was bringing Walt's wrath down on herself. "Tracy, don't . . ."

"You stay out of this, Nick," she yelled, then threw the second cooking kit at Walt, purposely missing him again.

Walt took a step toward her, then stopped, his interest caught by what she'd said. "What did I almost do, little girl?"

"You almost brought the whole countryside down on your stupid head, that's what," she said, praying she wasn't making things worse. "You think you're in some empty wilderness here, but I've got news for you, mister. This country is riddled with trappers and prospectors and hunters—most of them well-armed. They're all Mac's friends from years back. You make him mad, and he'll mobilize every last one of them to get you. And they will, believe me. They know this area, Walt. You don't. You harm either one of us and you won't get what you're after. You'll be a dead man. Or wish you were."

"Brave talk from a little girl," Walt said with a sneer. But a slight flicker of doubt had appeared in his flat gray eyes.

"Sensible talk from someone who knows Bill MacKay," Tracy said evenly. "He'll go totally crazy if you pull a stupid stunt like this, so why chance it? Why hand Mac body parts that could belong to anyone, for heaven's sake, when I can give you something that will prove you have us but won't send him into one of his blind rages? You'll get us all killed with your sick sadism."

Walt considered her remarks, then favored her with his sly smile. "Well then, for heaven's sake," he said, parroting her words. "Don't keep me waiting in suspense. Show me your big proof."

"It's in my bag back in the plane."

"This better not be some kind of cute trick," Walt warned after he'd sent Red down to the aircraft for the duffel bag.

"It's not a trick," she said with a pout. "I'm not the stupid one around here, remember?"

To her relief, Walt laughed at her insult. There was one advantage in being small—and blond, she thought. Men considered her harmless. They were wrong.

Nick watched in stunned amazement. Tracy was lying through her teeth and making Walt believe her. Mac flying into a blind rage? Total fiction. It might be true that he could mobilize all these hunters and prospectors she'd mentioned, but how? And to what end? Mac wouldn't take a chance on seeing Tracy hurt. He would do exactly as he was told if her safety was at stake.

Nick still couldn't quite figure how the fragile little creature had saved him from losing at least a couple of fingers. She'd flown at Walt, not giving a damn that the ax could hit her, and then she'd started berating the man as if *she* were holding the gun! At the moment she seemed about as fragile as a Sherman tank. What the hell had gotten into her? Despite the desperation of the circumstances, Nick almost smiled. Mac would have been proud of her—*he* certainly was.

When Red returned with the bag, Walt let Tracy dig inside it, but he aimed his gun straight at her heart to be sure she wouldn't try anything. Finally she pulled out a small multicolored rock and held it up.

Walt chewed on the inside corners of his mouth. "A pebble? That's your big proof?"

"This pebble," Tracy said archly, "happens to be an especially fine specimen of jasper conglomerate known colloquially as pudding stone." She frowned, wondering why she'd launched into a geology lesson. A touch of nerves, she supposed. Nick's fault. If only he'd stop staring at her, heating her blood with his penetrating gaze. "Anyway," she went on, "Mac polished this rock and gave it to me today just before I left him. All you have to do is show it to him, tell him you've got Nick and me, and say I begged him to pay whatever is asked to get us out. When he isn't provoked, Mac can be a reasonable man. Seeing this rock will worry him, but it won't trigger any heroic rescue action on his part. And be sure to remind him about my allergy."

"Allergy?" Walt repeated.

"To black flies." She injected a hint of barely controlled hysteria into her voice. "I react violently if I get too many bites. Once I nearly died. I'm sure Mac will think of that, but mention it just to be on the safe side."

"Okay, okay, I'll tell him. But, lady, this better work, or I'll come back here and slice off a few parts of you to persuade the old man."

Tracy's eyes widened at the ugly threat. "It'll work," she said firmly.

Walt finally took the rock. "Keep an eye on the girl while I'm gone, Red," he ordered. "But keep your hands off her. Time enough for a little fun later."

That's what you think, Tracy added silently.

Nick just kept watching her, wondering how she could remain so calm when she had to know Walt had just admitted he had no intention of letting either of them go once he'd gotten whatever ransom he was demanding. Their only chance was to escape while Walt was gone, and that hope was pitifully faint.

Tracy waited until Walt's plane was long gone before launching into her makeshift escape plot.

Looking around the room with undisguised distaste, she sighed heavily. "Okay, so I guess it's time for me to play housemaid. Is there a broom around here?"

"If you're thinkin' to start sweepin' and then swing a broom at me, forget it, lady. I ain't just off no turnip truck, you know."

Tracy thought Red was a little dull-witted to be entrusted with valuable prisoners. She was surprised Walt had hired him for the job. "How did you and Walt get together?" she asked, smiling at him. "Are you partners in crime?"

"He's my cousin," Red told her with obvious pride.

"And how did you come to be involved in this little caper of his?"

"You mean because I don't seem smart enough?"

Tracy's opinion of the man rose slightly. At least he knew his limitations. That was more than could be said for most people. "Are you smart enough, Red?" From the corner of her eye she could see Nick trying to free his hands. She wished he wouldn't. If Red spotted what he was up to, there was no telling what the man would do. Moving slowly and casually, pretending to examine the envelopes of dried food, she managed to get Red to turn enough so Nick was out of his line of vision. She repeated her question. "Do you think you're smart enough to pull off this job?"

"How smart do I need to be?" Red answered pragmatically. "I've got the gun, the guy's tied up, and even if you managed to make a run for it, where would you go?"

Tracy nodded. "You've got a point." Using the corner of a tattered gingham curtain to clean a spot on the blackened window, she peered outside and gave a theatrical shudder. "Lord, but it's spooky out there," she said, then looked at Red with pleading, frightened eyes. "We won't have to stay here overnight, will we? I couldn't bear it."

"Don't be such a sissy," Red said, slapping at his neck.

"The black flies are getting to you too," Tracy observed. "I hope you're not like me. Allergic, I mean."

"I'm not. I've been bitten plenty and I'm okay. Those sneaky little flies are just a nuisance, that's all."

"Maybe," Tracy agreed. "But I didn't know I was allergic until I woke up in the hospital with my hands and feet double their usual size and the doctor telling me I'd gone into a coma and hadn't been expected to live."

Red slapped at another fly that had gotten into his hair. "You tryna scare me? It won't work, y'know."

Tracy shrugged. "Suit yourself. But you don't have to put up with the nuisance of the little devils, Red. What kind of insect repellent are you using?"

Red showed her the bottle. "Supposed to be good stuff," he muttered.

"Commercial," Tracy said disdainfully. "Mac has a special brand made up. It's the only one that's ever worked for me. I have some in my bag. In fact, I ought to use it before I run into trouble." She went to her duffel bag and slowly took out the spray can, aware that Red's finger was on the trigger of his gun. He certainly wasn't a trusting soul, she thought as she sprayed a bit of the repellent into her palm and began smoothing it over her throat with long, slow strokes she hoped were seductive.

Nick watched, taut with anticipation. Tracy was planning something. Red was stupid, but he had the gun and wouldn't hesitate to use it on her. What was she up to? Surely she wasn't hoping to spray repellent into Red's eyes. Even he wouldn't fall for a sucker move like that.

All at once an unexpected stirring in his loins made Nick realize he was aroused by the way Tracy was applying the spray to her smooth skin, tipping her head back and closing her eyes. He tried to shake himself out of the spell she was casting, but the heat inside him was building and he could no longer deny the raw desire she'd triggered in him.

Nick was shocked at himself. He was no better than Red, who at the moment was leaning toward Tracy, his eyes bulging, his mouth agape.

She opened her eyes and sprayed her body, careful to make no threatening motion toward Red. Glancing at Nick, she was momentarily distracted from her main goal. Unbelievably Nick's eyes were dark with desire. Amazed, she turned away with a smile. So that was all she had to do to get Nick's attention, she thought. Tie him to a chair in a life-threatening situation and start putting on bug spray. Why hadn't she thought of that a long time ago?

Back to business, she told herself, turning once again to Red and smiling. "You're about to get another bite," she informed him. "On your forehead.

Goodness, these miserable little monsters go after you, don't they?"

As Red slapped at the nonexistent black fly, Tracy stepped to one side so the gun was no longer trained directly on her.

Nick watched, holding his breath, knowing what was coming yet not daring to hope she could pull it off without getting herself shot.

"You missed," she told Red, adding helpfully, "Now the beast is after your ear. Here . . . let me at him." And as Nick broke into a cold sweat, Red actually sat there smiling while Tracy raised the spray can and let him have it full in the face.

He shrieked and began flailing with his gun while foolishly rubbing the chemical further into his eyes with his free hand.

In a lightning-quick move, Tracy grabbed the handles of her duffel bag, assumed a batter's stance, and swung, connecting with Red's skull. Nick remembered how she'd tucked her Dickens anthology into the bag on the plane. Had she been planning ahead even then, he wondered. Whether or not she had, the lady was formidable. She'd only stunned Red, so she was taking another swing. It knocked him facedown on the floor, his gun still in his hand until Tracy stepped on his wrist and deftly removed the weapon. Moving out of his reach, she pointed the pistol at the dazed but conscious man. "Now, you just stay where you are, all right?" she said in her sweet voice. "Don't move, because if you do, I'll shoot you. I promise."

A moment later she was beside Nick, still holding the gun on Red while undoing a knot with her free hand.

"Not bad," Nick said with a feeble grin. "You're Mac's kid all right."

Tracy beamed at the compliment but didn't take her eyes off Red for a second. She hoped he wouldn't move. She didn't want to shoot him.

Once Nick was free she gave him the gun.

He tucked it into his waistband, rubbed his wrists, then took the rope and thoroughly hog-tied Red.

"Walt's gonna kill me for this," Red said. "But you still ain't out of the woods, y'know."

"Cute," Tracy remarked as she dumped out the contents of her duffel bag and began repacking it with what she considered the new essentials. "There's extra rope, Nick. Could you make a sling so I can carry the sleeping bag on my back? I'll let you take the duffel bag; it's going to be kind of heavy." She tossed in the boy scout cooking gear and the food envelopes, then picked up a couple of cans of beans and looked at Nick questioningly. "Should we take these? They'll add weight but we might be glad to have them."

Nick took the cans from her and put them into the bag, then tested the weight. "It's fine," he said. "Not too heavy at all."

As he went back to fashioning the sleeping bag carrier, Tracy returned her first aid and emergency kit to the duffel, hesitated, then added a lightweight but essential toiletry and cosmetic pouch. If she was going to have Nick all to herself in the forest, she wasn't about to leave vanity behind completely.

Picking up the can of repellent, Tracy handed it to Nick. "You'd better put some of this on," she suggested, adding with a mischievous grin, "But spray it into your hand first. You wouldn't want to get that stuff in your eyes."

Nick stared at her as if seeing her for the first time. "Good advice," he said huskily. "I'll keep it in mind."

Realizing Walt had flown off with Nick's suitcase, Tracy rifled through her clothes to find her windbreaker and long-sleeved sweatshirt. "This jacket should fit you, Nick," she said as she tossed it to him. "At the moment you don't need it for warmth, but even in August it's a good idea to cover as much of your skin as possible for protection against flies and mosquitoes."

He put the light brown jacket on and grinned at her. "Kind of big for you, isn't it?"

Pulling the yellow sweatshirt over her head, Tracy laughed. "I like my sportswear roomy," she explained.

Nick couldn't stop grinning. She looked ridiculously adorable, her tiny body lost in her "roomy" sweatshirt. Then his smile faded abruptly. "Will that thing and the spray protect you enough? Are you sure we should run for it, Tracy? What about your allergy?"

She frowned, then remembered. "Oh, that." With a shrug, she chuckled quietly. "I'm not allergic to black flies or anything else." Indicating Red, she rolled her eyes. "Except maybe him."

Red, finally realizing he'd been thoroughly hoodwinked, howled out a protest, calling Tracy several choice names.

"Watch your mouth, Red," Nick warned the man. "It isn't polite to insult a lady."

The soft, almost casual menace in Nick's voice quieted Red. Nick positioned the sleeping bag on Tracy's back, then slid his arms through the straps of the makeshift backpack he'd fashioned out of the duffel bag and reached for the ax.

Pleased, Tracy realized that Nick's innate common sense made him competent in any setting. It was one of the many things she admired about him. Only then did it hit her that during the whole crisis she'd forgotten her paralyzing shyness with Nick. "All set?" she asked with a smile.

Nick grinned, opened the door and gave her a slightly awkward, courtly bow. "After you, milady," he said.

Tracy stepped out into the cool, clean northern air and took a deep, soothing breath. Only now that she knew they were safe did she begin trembling.

Newly attuned to Tracy, Nick noticed the change in her. She wasn't quite as calm as she'd been. Once again he was overcome by an urge to hold and comfort her—and by other, unfamiliar feelings toward her—but there was no time. "You okay?" he asked, unable to keep the concern out of his tone.

"I'm fine," she stated firmly. "Let's go."

"Sure," he agreed, following her and finding her pace amazingly fast. "But where? I'm afraid Red might have been right, Tracy. We're definitely not out of the woods. I'm no bushman, I hate to admit. We could end up walking in circles and getting nowhere."

Turning, Tracy gave him a brilliant smile he knew he would remember for the rest of his life. "Don't worry, Nick," she told him. "Why, I was born and bred in this briar patch."

Four

"I don't get it," Nick said after they'd stopped to drink from a small freshwater stream.

Tracy was kneeling beside the bubbling water, filling the canteen she'd taken from the backpack. "Don't get what?"

"We've just walked nonstop for an hour. I like to think I'm in pretty good shape, but it's all I can do to keep up with you," Nick admitted. "You don't pause to decide which direction to take even when we have to detour to go around difficult terrain. Yet you don't seem to be wandering aimlessly, just trying to put some distance between us and that cabin."

Tracy straightened up, recapped the canteen, and returned it to the pack. "I use landmarks. Same as back home, Nick. When you're on a city street and want to go south, you don't stop every little while to check your direction. You simply adjust and keep going."

Nick looked around at the dense, seemingly endless forest. "Oh, sure. Simple," he said sardonically.

Tracy chuckled. "I guess to you the trees all look the same at first glance, but not to me. When we left the cabin, I knew we wanted to head south—"

"Question," Nick interrupted. "How did you know even that much?"

"Because Walt flew northeast when he should have been taking us southwest," Tracy replied, opening a package of trail mix she'd found among the dried food envelopes. "Want some of this?"

He held out one hand and she shook some of the dried fruit and nuts into his cupped palm. "Okay, let's back up a little further, then," Nick persisted. "How did you know Walt was heading the wrong way?"

Tracy perched herself on a rock as though settling into a lounge chair. "I wasn't sure it was the *wrong* way," she answered. "Just not the way I'd expected to go. With the benefit of hindsight I realize now I should have been more suspicious than I was, but I'd been too—" She stopped short of admitting to Nick she'd been too addled by the prospect of being alone with him to think clearly. "I have this problem," she went on instead. "It's hard for me to tell a person I think he's doing something wrong. Mac says I'm sometimes polite to a fault, and this was one of those times. I kept telling myself I was mixed up about the direction and had no right to question a seasoned pilot like Walt."

Hunkering down cross-legged on the ground opposite Tracy, Nick grinned. "You managed to shed that politeness once you knew what was going on." In a more serious tone he added, "You scared hell out of me, Tracy. I kept expecting Walt to lose his temper and shut you up the hard way."

Tracy looked at Nick unbelievingly. Had he really been worried about her, or was she reading too much into a simple remark? She brought herself up short: Of *course* he'd been worried about her. He was a decent, caring man who would worry about anyone in the same situation. "More trail mix?" she asked, leaning toward him and holding out the packet, trying not to tremble. The intimacy of being alone in the quiet forest with Nick and having their first companionable chat in all the time they'd been acquainted was getting to her.

Nick accepted another handful. "Anyway, you still haven't told me how you knew we were flying the wrong way," he said. "You seemed to be looking out the window a lot and then glancing at your watch."

"When I was a kid Mac taught me to tell direction with pretty good accuracy by the position of the sun in relation to time."

"I'm a city dweller," Nick remarked. "To me the sun has two positions: above the skyscrapers or behind them."

Tracy was delighted at Nick's lack of pretense. "At least you're not a know-it-all," Tracy said with a grin. She got to her feet and reached for the sleeping bag she'd put down earlier.

Nick stood up to help her. "I gather we're forging ahead," he said, adjusting the rope sling over Tracy's slender shoulders. As his fingers accidentally grazed the back of her neck, she gave a tiny, involuntary shudder that puzzled him. Did she dislike his touch, or had she felt the same current of electricity that had just buzzed through his body?

"Thanks," Tracy said in a small voice, her whole being acutely alive as her long-buried desire for Nick surfaced in the form of a hot tingling that spread to every inch of her skin. After a long moment, she sighed. "We really should keep going. Walt said he'd be back soon. He might come looking for us, so the more ground we can cover the better."

"Are we trying to reach the lodge or a nearby town?" Nick asked vaguely, still confused by his body's response to Tracy. His feelings for her kept growing. He'd told himself the flash of desire he'd felt back at the cabin could be chalked up to circumstance: intense fear was a notorious aphrodisiac. But what about the rush of excitement he'd experienced at the simple act of brushing his hand against her neck? That didn't make sense at all.

Tracy had forgotten to answer Nick. Watching him shrug into the straps of the backpack, she'd lost herself in the pleasure of his graceful movements, the curl of dark chest hair at the base of his throat, the inviting sensuality of his wonderful mouth. Belatedly she recalled he'd asked her something. "I beg your pardon?" she said a little breathlessly.

Nick stared at her in shock, the desire mounting within him intensified by the incredible darkening of her eyes. It was like gazing into a whole new universe, a vista of unfamiliar galaxies. "What?" he murmured.

Tracy bit down on her lower lip, utterly disoriented.

Nick wondered why he'd never noticed before how soft and full and sweetly pink Tracy's mouth was. Hardly aware he was moving, he took a step toward her. "Tracy . . ."

She panicked. He looked as if he planned to kiss her, and the prospect was as terrifying as it was tempting. If Nick even once took her in his arms, if his mouth moved over hers in what surely would be for him a casual pleasure—or worse, some kind of misplaced display of gratitude—she would never be the same Tracy Carlisle again. If she gave in to her hunger for Nick now, it would become all-consuming long after they would return to their normal lives. "You asked whether we were trying for the lodge or for a town," she suddenly remembered aloud, talking very fast. "Neither. All we need to do is head south until we hit the railroad tracks."

Nick blinked as sanity slowly returned. What was happening to him? Had he really just been on the verge of kissing Tracy Carlisle? "And then what?" he asked, trying to regain his composure.

"Then we flag down the train and take it to the next town," she said, turning to head back to the trail.

They walked for another hour. At the sound of gurgling water, Tracy paused partway down a hill. "Ready for our next break?" she asked lightly.

Nick almost laughed aloud. Ready? He felt like collapsing then and there. The straps of the backpack were cutting into his shoulders, he was sweating, and his legs were growing heavier with every step. Yet there was no way he would admit that keeping up with Tracy was killing him. "Whatever you say," he answered nonchalantly.

Tracy followed the bubbling noises to a brook several yards to the right of where they'd been walking. She dropped the sleeping bag gratefully and rolled her shoulders several times to loosen her cramped muscles.

Nick leaned the ax against a tree and slid the backpack to the ground. "Like I said," he conceded,

"I thought I was in pretty good shape, but this little hike is telling me otherwise."

Tracy knelt to dip her hands in the stream and splashed the cooling water over her face and neck. "You're in *great* shape," she said as Nick joined her. Embarrassed by her small outburst, she cleared her throat. "I mean, it's just that you're probably using a different set of muscles from those you normally use."

"And you?" he asked as he thoroughly splashed himself, then raked his fingers through his dampened hair. "I suppose treks like this are part of your normal routine?"

"Not recently," Tracy said ingenuously. "But they used to be when I spent more time with Mac. Anyway, I'm feeling the effects of this walk myself. It's pretty rough going. If I don't appear worn out, it's because I learned early on that if I couldn't keep up with Mac, I wouldn't get to go with him on weekends."

A vivid picture popped into Nick's head of Mac striding through the woods with a tiny, towheaded bundle of determination struggling along behind him. The tug to his heart was just another in a long series of shocks he'd had since Tracy had joined him on the dock at Sunstone Lake a few hours earlier.

To mask the confused welter of emotions hitting him, he chug-a-lugged two full cups of water from the stream, then looked at the empty cup with a frown. "I guess you're sure this stuff is safe to drink."

"Better than the chemical soup passing for water in most cities," Tracy answered, lying back against the hill, suppressing a groan of relief as the soft, mossy undergrowth cushioned her aching bones.

She clasped her hands behind her head and closed her eyes as she spoke again. "I love the taste of it, don't you?"

Nick was helping himself to a third cup. "Come to think of it, I guess I do," he agreed. "You want some more?"

"Not yet," she murmured. "I'd just like to relax for a couple of minutes, okay?"

"Good idea," Nick said, stretching out under the shade of a nearby tree. "I think I'll join you."

Tracy's eyes snapped open. When she saw that Nick was several feet away, she realized how foolish her edginess was making her. He hadn't meant anything untoward, like lying beside her, wrapping his arms around her, capturing her lips with his, and pressing his body into hers. How silly she was to think such a thing.

Sighing, she closed her eyes again and, just for a moment, surrendered to silly dreams.

Neither of them spoke for several minutes.

Nick couldn't remember when he'd experienced such a sense of peace. With his eyes shut he focused on the subtle sounds of the forest: the gurgling water, the distant tapping of a woodpecker, the rustling noises made by small animals in the undergrowth, or the rising breeze as it played among the tree branches. Opening his eyes again, he mentally traced the intricate patterns of leaves, dark against the gray-blue sky and fluttering like winged creatures trying to break free.

A phalanx of clouds was moving in, and Nick could almost smell the coming rain, the elusive scent mingled with pine and mint and sweetgrass.

Raising himself to a half-sitting position with his

weight resting on his elbows, he took advantage of Tracy's closed eyes to study her. After all he'd seen her do, she still struck him as fragile, but not like the crystal he'd compared her to once. She was more like . . . what? He spied a small blossom on the forest floor, its petals almost translucently white, so delicate it looked as if a breath of wind would destroy it. Yet it was hardy enough to survive and bloom, surrounded by thistles and wild grasses and gnarled tree roots. Tracy was like that flower.

He'd always prided himself on being a canny judge of people. How could he have been so wrong about her? So far off base?

He didn't even seem to know himself. After a trek that had worn him out, a woman should have been the last thing on his mind, yet he wanted Tracy, wanted her as he'd never wanted anyone, even though he'd been telling himself for three years that she was totally undesirable—too slender, not voluptuous enough for his taste, too . . . perfect. He'd thought of her as an exquisite porcelain figurine, not as a flesh-and-blood woman. Had he been crazy? Or was he crazy now?

He had to curb his feelings. That much he knew. Tracy—the Tracy he was coming to know—deserved better than a passionate interlude. And that's all it would be if he made love to her. All it *could* be. Nick Corcoran wasn't about to forget that he was headed for the top, and he was going to get what he wanted honestly, not by romancing the boss's granddaughter the way some of his colleagues stupidly hoped to do. A couple of them had even made empty boasts about marrying Tracy as a shortcut to heading Mac's empire.

Not Nick Corcoran. He didn't need to use a woman to get what he wanted.

There was no question about it: Tracy Carlisle was off limits to him—and his unruly body had better pay attention to that fact.

Tracy opened her eyes and looked straight into the burning depths of Nick's hazel eyes. "I thought you were resting," she blurted out as she sat up.

"I was," he answered, caught off guard. "We're going to get some rain, aren't we?" The weather again, he thought. They always went back to discussing the weather.

"Looks that way," Tracy agreed, forcing herself to her feet. She looked at her watch. "It's nearly five o'clock. Maybe we can get in another hour of walking before we have to stop for the night. Are you game?"

"I am if you are." Nick got up and refilled the small canteen they'd emptied during their hike.

He was dreading the night ahead. His body wasn't paying a whit of attention to the orders from his brain. If anything, the desire building inside him was growing more hot and urgent. How was he going to get through a night alone in the forest with this woman without dragging her into his arms and just taking her? The primitive setting was no help, he mused as he filled the cup with water, leaned forward, and dumped the contents over his head.

"You're that hot?" Tracy asked, watching him.

With water streaming down his face, he straightened up and looked steadily at her. "I'm that hot," he muttered.

"You're sure you want to keep going, then?"

"I'm sure."

Tracy shrugged and picked up the sleeping bag. A moment later she was frowning, wondering whether her imagination was playing tricks on her or Nick's hands were actually trembling as he helped her with the rope sling.

"What do you use as landmarks?" he asked as they started off again. He had to try to make light conversation, at least for a while, to force his imagination away from the direction it was taking as Tracy's trim hips swayed provocatively in front of him.

It took her a moment to comprehend his question. "Anything," she said at last. "But I usually pick three and line them up. For instance, there's a big rotted-out tree stump behind us. Then, straight ahead, there's a white birch with a branch half off, probably struck by lightning recently. Beyond that there's a huge blue spruce so distinctive, it's like the World Trade Center Buildings: you just wouldn't mistake them for anything else. See it?"

Nick nodded. "Right. Hey, that's interesting," he said sincerely. "Until you pointed out those individual characteristics just now it was all a big green blur to me."

"The first time I hit New York it was a big concrete blur to me," Tracy said with a smile.

"Point taken," Nick conceded. "Now, let's see. I guess as soon as we hit the birch we pick a landmark beyond the spruce."

"Exactly. Easy, huh?"

"Too easy," Nick remarked. "If finding your way in the woods is that simple, how come so many people get lost?"

"Panic, mainly. Forgetting to use their brains."

Tracy stopped talking again to give her full attention to negotiating a path down a short but steep and rocky incline. She waited for Nick to follow. "You want to hear something crazy?" he said impulsively. "I'm actually enjoying myself. Why have I always turned down Mac's invitations to spend a few days with him in the bush? I think I've been missing something."

It was all Tracy could do not to fling herself into his arms and hug him. "You're a good sport," she said, chuckling.

Feeling unexpectedly close to Tracy thanks to their silly banter, Nick reached out to grasp her arm, stopping her in her tracks and turning her to face him. "I said I was enjoying myself, and I meant it," he stated almost fiercely. Seeing her startled expression, he softened his tone. "I'm getting to know a Tracy Carlisle I never knew before. I'm discovering a whole new beautiful world. We're free, thanks to you. I still have all my fingers, thanks to you. And we're not even lost, also thanks to you. And you say *I'm* a good sport?" Releasing her arm, he trailed the backs of his fingers over her cheek. "You're mighty easy to please, Tracy."

Tracy's body instantly was suffused with warmth, her pulse raced, her heart pounded, her breath quickened. Nick's eyes seemed to reflect the rich deep green of the forest and flicker with inner golden flames that hypnotized her; his voice held a gentle quality she'd never heard before, and his touch was soft and mesmerizing. Her fears forgotten, she was captured in a spell she hoped would never be broken. Easy to please, she repeated silently, wanting to tell him how much he pleased her by his mere existence. Yet she couldn't form the words.

He asked the question that had been on his mind throughout the afternoon. "Why did you do it, Tracy?"

"Do what?" she whispered, barely able to speak.

"Risk your life for me? Throw yourself at Walt without any thought for your own safety?"

She lowered her eyelids, not sure what to say.

"Look at me," Nick said, barely restraining himself from brushing his lips over the dark, curved fringe of lashes veiling her eyes. "Look at me, Tracy. Tell me why you did it."

When she opened her eyes, the impact of their brilliant blue took Nick's breath away. "You're so beautiful," he whispered. "Why do you have to be so damned beautiful?"

Tracy was convinced she had lapsed back into a dream. To hear Nick say she was beautiful was so much more than she'd ever hoped for, she hardly dared believe it. Instinctively she parted her lips, longing for his kiss.

The hum of an aircraft engine overhead shattered the moment. There had been two other planes during the afternoon, but this one was making a descent toward the lake Nick and Tracy had left behind.

"Walt can't see us from the air," Tracy said aloud. "The forest cover is too thick. But he might try when he finds out we've gotten away."

"What about tracking us?" Nick asked, reluctantly lowering his hand, his fingertips feeling cheated out of touching the silk of her skin. "On the ground, I mean. You think he might try that?"

Tracy shook her head. "I doubt that he has the skills. It would take an expert to follow our trail all this way. I think we're safe enough now. That isn't what's worrying me."

Nick understood. His thoughts were going in the same direction. "Mac," he said quietly.

"Mac," Tracy repeated. "I'm sure he's playing some cat-and-mouse game with Walt until he knows what's really happening, but . . ." Her eyes filled with tears, and a hard knot of terror settled at the pit of her stomach. "I'm scared, Nick," she said, her voice breaking. Drawing a shaky breath, she struggled for control, covering her face with her hands. "I'm sorry," she whispered. "I'll pull myself together, I promise. It's just that . . ." She pressed her fingers against her eyelids as if she could push back the tears, took another deep breath, and lowered her hands. "Okay," she said as firmly as possible, forcing herself to remember all the lessons Mac had taught her about dealing with fear. "Okay," she repeated with more strength. "Being scared doesn't help, right? It doesn't help us, doesn't help Mac. Being smart is what counts, and you can't be smart if you panic, can you?"

Afraid she was finally beginning to come apart at the seams and wrenched by the anguish that had gripped her, Nick started to reach for Tracy.

She moved away and turned to face him. "I'm fine now," she said with a defiant lift to her chin. "Sorry about that little lapse." She took a deep breath and squared her shoulders. "Let's get this show on the road, shall we?"

Five

For nearly an hour Walt's plane had been circling overhead like a menacing hawk.

Nick noticed a break in the line of trees ahead. "I hope that's not a clearing," he said.

Tracy looked back at him, then up at the Cessna. "Probably a lake," she said, scowling. "Walt must be almost as dumb as Red—or figures *we* are—if he imagines we'll come out from the cover of the forest. What does he think we'll do, go for a swim?"

Within minutes the gray-blue waters of a lake were in sight, and Tracy stopped on the tree-sheltered path to look around, listening. "Over there," she said after a moment, pointing to the right.

Nick followed without question, perfectly satisfied by now that Tracy knew what she was doing.

"We can make camp right here," she said when they'd reached a stream that fed the lake. She dropped the sleeping bag, glancing at Nick as he put down the ax and the backpack. "That thing must feel like it's loaded with bricks," she said in sympathy, kneeling by the spring to splash herself liberally with icy water. "I still say you're a good sport, if only for not complaining."

Privately Nick thought the pack felt as if it were stuffed with concrete pilings, though he wouldn't say so. He was flattered by Tracy's admiration. But he did have one suggestion. "Let's eat the beans. I'm hungry enough to be glad to have them, but I won't miss the weight of those cans." Deciding he wasn't likely to need the gun for a while, he took it from his waistband and slipped it into an outside pocket of the backpack.

"Sit on that big boulder," Tracy said impulsively. "I'll massage your shoulders."

Nick was only too glad to comply. When Tracy's surprisingly strong fingers worked at his neck and shoulder muscles, he groaned with pleasure. "I'll return the favor," he promised. "You must be hurting too."

Standing behind him, she smiled, glad her concern for him had made her forget her shyness. Touching him was sheer pleasure as she felt the warmth and strength of his body through his clothes. "The sleeping bag wasn't heavy," she said.

"I'm going to do it anyway," Nick insisted, bowing his head to give her more access to his neck muscles. "That rope sling I made was digging into your shoulders, and don't try to pretend it wasn't. I saw the way you kept trying to shift it back and forth to distribute the pain evenly."

Tracy laughed. Nick was right, but she was surprised he'd noticed her discomfort—surprised and pleased. And sorely tempted to slide her fingers inside the collar of his shirt, to bend and touch her lips to the nape of his neck, to let her thighs press against his back as she stood close behind him.

"I was just thinking," Nick said, his voice slightly husky as he battled another wave of desire that had gripped him. "We should be glad Cooper is up there searching for us. It means he's determined to recapture us. He's not going to do anything rash—for instance, turn on Mac—until we're back in tow. And remember, a kidnapper's not about to harm the guy who's supposed to pay the ransom."

Tracy's hands suddenly were stilled as she took in Nick's words. "You're right. Dear heaven, you're right." Tears stung her eyelids. "Thank you," she said softly. "I hadn't thought of that. I don't know what's wrong with me, Nick. I'm trying to keep my mind clear, but whenever I think of anything happening to my grandfather, I just seize up. I can't get past the fear to see the logic. How can I be any good to Mac that way?"

Touched by the quiet desperation in Tracy's voice, Nick twisted around so he could pull her into his lap and cradle her, gently but firmly pushing her head down onto his shoulder. "You're too hard on yourself," he said, absently kissing her forehead. "You've given all three of us the only chance we had to get out of this mess: you got the two of us into the forest, and you know how to get us safely out of it. Have faith, Tracy—in yourself, in Mac, in me. We're going to be fine, honey. There's no question. We're going to make it."

"I know," she murmured, taking comfort from Nick's calm strength, only vaguely noticing how natural it felt to be in his arms, hearing him call her honey. Had it been only earlier in the morning that he'd spoken so gruffly to her, glared at her? "I'm grateful not to be alone in this," she admitted. "But it's awful for you to be dragged into something by sheer bad luck. You weren't supposed to be in that plane, and now your life is in danger just because Mac asked you to travel with me."

"I wouldn't have it any other way," Nick said with a gentle smile, meaning every word. The thought of Tracy being in danger by herself made him feel sick. His arms tightened around her as he realized how much she'd come to mean to him in a few short hours.

Yet was that true? Had his feelings for her changed only hours before? He thought back to the first moments when the danger had become evident. Hadn't his first reaction been to take care of Tracy, to protect her from harm?

His mind went back even further, to times when some of Sunstone's backstabbing employees had sharpened their knives and aimed them at Tracy. Hadn't he leapt to her defense? Hadn't his anger at their sneak attacks been a bit misplaced considering how little he'd supposedly liked her?

Just how long had he cared for Tracy Carlisle subconsciously, he wondered.

"Your turn," he said, abruptly deciding it was time for her neck rub. Easily lifting her as he stood up, he turned and deposited her on the boulder, then went around to stand behind her and began making circles with his thumbs along the tight cords of her shoulders.

Tracy knew there was no point in protesting. Besides, she didn't want to, she realized. Nick's strong fingers were gently soothing not only her tired body but her whole being. "That's . . . so . . . nice," she said, closing her eyes.

"Good," Nick said in a low voice that was a balm to her taut nerves. "Just relax, honey. Let go. You've been taking care of both of us all day. Now it's my turn to take care of you, so you don't have to think or worry or be afraid."

Gradually Tracy released her tensions and felt an inner peace settle over her. She was contented, confident of the future.

Nick's thoughts were troubled. He knew this adventure wouldn't really change anything for him. His ambition would take top priority in his life, leaving no room for a serious relationship with anyone. Tracy would still be the rival who might beat him out for control of Sunstone. Or, if he had his way, she would be the heiress deprived by one Nick Corcoran of her succession to power. How was he ever going to square those realities with the new reality of his feelings for Tracy and hers for him? "Better?" he asked, suddenly dropping his hands and moving away from her with a strained smile.

It took Tracy just seconds to gather her wits and her control about her like a protective mantle. Something had shattered the mood, driving Nick away from her again. "Much," she answered brightly. "Thanks." Looking up at the sky, she said, "I'm amazed it hasn't rained."

The weather again, Nick thought.

Lifting her chin, Tracy took a deep breath, bit down on her tremulous lower lip, and picked up the ax.

Nick grinned and shook his head, moved by her

unique mixture of spunk and vulnerability. All of a sudden he didn't care about corporate rivalries or the complications of life. Nothing mattered but Tracy.

When she began swinging the ax with startling expertise, lopping off branches of a sprawling evergreen, Nick spoke firmly. "Stop it, Tracy."

She sliced off one more branch, then turned to look questioningly at him. "Stop what?"

He walked over to her, took the ax, and leaned it against the tree. "Stop what you're doing. I admit I'm a tenderfoot, but I'm perfectly capable of using that particular implement. Even city boys sometimes have to chop wood. For fireplaces, you know." He curved his hands around her shoulders and smiled down at her. "Now, did you have a practical reason for the violence you were visiting upon that tree, or is that the way you deal with your emotions?"

Tracy stared at him for a moment, then had to laugh. "Both," she admitted. "That tree's a balsam. The branches make a wonderful bed." She hesitated, then went on a bit raggedly, finding it difficult to discuss the night's accommodations with Nick. "Um . . . I thought . . . I thought you should use the sleeping bag and the ground sheet that's in my emergency kit. I can wrap myself up in these branches."

"Not a chance, sweetheart," Nick flatly replied.

"But I'm used to that sort of bed," Tracy argued. "And you carried the heavy pack. You'll be all bent over tomorrow if you aren't careful."

"Fine," Nick stated. "I'll do my Quasimodo number. But I will not take the sleeping bag and leave you to a bunch of balsam branches. I have my own ideas on this subject, if you'd care to hear them."

Tracy wasn't sure, but she nodded.

Nick drew her a little closer to him, imprisoning her gaze with his own. "We'll make a mattress from the balsam. A double-sized mattress."

Tracy swallowed hard, anticipating what was coming.

"Then we'll spread your ground sheet over it," Nick went on, each word a gentle caress. "We'll open up the sleeping bag to make a quilt that will cover us both." He brought her nearer, speaking very softly. "And then I'll hold you all night long, Tracy. My shoulder will be your pillow, and I'll keep you close to me so I'll know you're warm and safe." He slid his arms around her and continued holding her gaze.

Mesmerized, Tracy couldn't have moved if she'd wanted to. She didn't want to. Neither could she breathe as Nick's head descended with excruciating slowness, his lips just brushing hers. . . .

A sudden explosion split the air. Nick's arms became iron bands around Tracy as he threw her to the ground and covered her body with his own, cursing himself for leaving the gun in the backpack.

They stayed that way for several seconds while Nick tried to think of a way to get to the gun yet keep protecting Tracy. "Walt's still overhead," he muttered. "He must have spotted us after all and told Red how to track us."

Tracy frowned. That was impossible.

Another cracking sound, a loud swish, and a soft thud made Nick stiffen but reassured Tracy. "A tree branch," she told him. "That was lightning hitting a tree. The noise just now was the branch breaking off and falling to the ground. Red isn't out there, Nick. And Walt can't spot us." Suddenly overwhelmed by Nick's instinctive protectiveness, she looked up at him with shining eyes. "You shielded me with your own body," she whispered.

Nick realized he'd done just that but felt a little silly about his misplaced heroism. "What was I saying about not being a tenderfoot? I could have sworn that was a gunshot. You're sure it wasn't?"

"I'm sure. I ought to have known right away, but I guess I'm a bit edgy today." She cradled his face in her hands. "You asked me why I risked myself to spare you. Now I'm asking you the same thing, Nick."

He searched the infinite azure depths of her eyes. "I guess there are some feelings inside both of us we've kept under wraps," he answered at last. Then he smiled. "But some things won't stay suppressed forever. This, for instance." Lowering his head, he grazed his lips over Tracy's, then deepened the kiss, discovering her soft textures, her sweetness and warmth.

Tracy was dizzy with pleasure, overwhelmed by sensation. Nick's kiss was even more wonderful than in her fantasies, his lips warm and firm as they moved over hers, his tongue gentle yet thorough.

She laced her fingers through his hair and pressed her body upward into his, instinctively rotating her hips against him and exulting in the heated, thrusting response that was restrained only by the layers of clothing between them.

Nick gasped with rising excitement at each of Tracy's rhythmic motions. Lifting himself slightly, he rested his weight on one elbow while his free hand learned the contours of her body, her breasts, her slender waist, her stomach, her thighs, the gentle mound at their apex.

With a sharp intake of breath Tracy thrust herself against his hand. She arched her back as he smoothed his palm upward, searing her skin, setting fires inside her. "Touch me, Nick," she urged. "I need you to touch me."

Understanding, he pushed his hand under her T-shirt and closed his eyes to concentrate on the pleasure of feeling the cool satin of her skin at his fingertips.

He encountered a bra but pushed its lacy cup aside, filling his palm with Tracy's sweetly rounded breast, at the same time capturing her mouth in a deep, demanding kiss.

Thunder rolled in the distance and lightning cracked again, but neither Nick nor Tracy cared. They were oblivious to everything but touching and tasting each other, eagerly giving in to a passion that had exploded with so much power, they both knew it had been building between them for a very long time.

Nick could feel the swollen tip of Tracy's breast against his palm. He wanted to feel it in his mouth, to tease it to undreamed-of heights with his teeth and lips and tongue, then move to her other soft mound and bring it to rosy fullness the same way.

Still resting his weight on one elbow, he pushed Tracy's shirt up and was about to dip his head to pleasure himself with her velvety sweetness when a drop of rain splashed on her forehead. Then another bounced off her nose.

"Oh, no," Tracy said. "Why did it have to start *now*! What rotten timing!"

She and Nick looked at each other in dismay and burst out laughing. He got to his feet and helped her up, then pulled her back into his arms under the shelter of a tree. "Hell," he said, still laughing. "But I'm the one with lousy timing, not the weather. I've had three years to take off my blinders, three years to kiss you this way and make love to you. So I had to wait until some nut is trying to get his hands on us while we're racing to get to a railroad and flag down a train. I had all afternoon to enjoy you, and I waited until the storm decided to let loose." Nuzzling into Tracy's damp neck, he hoped the rain would cool him off. He couldn't take much more frustration. "I certainly didn't choose my moment very well."

With a regretful chuckle Tracy tilted back her head and once again cradled his face in her hands as she gazed up at him, her eyes heavy-lidded. "But you didn't choose the moment, Nick."

He showered gentle kisses on her forehead and brows and the corners of her eyes. "That's true," he conceded, licking a raindrop from her cheek. "I guess it chose us."

"But you're right," Tracy said, realizing they had to give in to the unavoidable. "We do have to make camp," she reminded him. "Getting caught in a bit of rain is funny now, but it won't feel so great after we're soaked to the skin, freezing and hungry and miserable."

Reluctantly Nick released her. "You do make a case for putting duty first, ma'am."

Tracy laughed again and realized that she'd been laughing quite a lot, considering the circumstances. "I'll get going on a campfire if you'll cut some wood before you start shearing off those balsam branches for our"—she smiled happily—"our bed." Glancing at the trees around them, she pointed to a spruce a few feet away. "The bottom branches of that tree will burn beautifully. It's time to prove you city boys really do know your stuff when it comes to firewood."

"How do you plan to start a fire under these conditions?" he asked as he picked up the ax and prepared to rise to her challenge. Merely curious, he had no doubt that Tracy could manage it. He also didn't question the wisdom of building a fire with Walt Cooper still flying in low circles above them. If Tracy felt it was safe, it was safe.

She strolled over to a birch tree and began removing strips of bark. "A fire's no problem," she answered. "Birch bark is so full of oils you can actually dip it in water and it'll still burn. Besides, one of the reasons I wanted to stop here was that I noticed a perfect spot for a fire, right over there on that slope of rock with the overhang that shelters it so nicely."

Nick had another thought. "Neither of us smokes. What about matches? Don't tell me you know how to rub sticks together to make sparks."

"As a matter of fact, I do," she said, thinking she didn't need sticks of wood or anything else besides Nick Corcoran's presence to make sparks. "Mac gave me a thorough education in the art of wilderness survival under the most primitive conditions," she explained. "But he also taught me some simpler skills. Like carrying an emergency kit. Mine has wooden matches in a waterproof case." She grinned. "I don't leave home without it."

"I should have known," Nick said with a roll of his eyes as he wondered whether Tracy would ever cease to amaze him. "What else do you have in your little bag of tricks, sweetheart?"

She loved his endearments, was warmed by them as if a fire already were burning. Taking her curls of birch bark to the sloping rock, she put them down and then began gathering dry twigs and branches. "What else do I have? Let's see. The ground sheet I mentioned earlier. It's made of some sort of space-age material that folds down as small and light as a silk scarf. A little flashlight . . ."

"Does it work?" Nick asked as he established a smooth rhythm for cutting the firewood.

"Of course it works," she said. "I check it regularly. To quote Red, I didn't just fall off no turnip truck, y'know."

Nick laughed at her mimicry. "Go on, Tracy. Is there anything else in your kit?"

"I have flares," she went on, pausing in her work for a moment to enjoy the play of Nick's muscles as he smoothly swung the ax. Then she shook herself. What had she been talking about? Flares. "We can use them if Walt ever leaves and a plane I definitely recognize as belonging to someone friendly goes over. There's also—"

"Wait a minute," Nick interrupted. "How can you definitely recognize a plane as belonging to someone friendly? How could you be sure it wasn't Walt in a different one or another pilot he'd brought in to help him?"

"The bush pilots I know have pretty distinctive planes," Tracy explained.

"Just how much time have you spent in this country?" Nick asked, his curiosity piqued all over again.

"Most of my summers from the time I was a kid until I finished college, including some stints as a tree planter," Tracy answered, putting her kindling on the rock and dropping to one knee to arrange a small circle of birch-bark curls. "And a week or two whenever I could manage it once I started working. Whatever time I could steal I tried to spend at the lodge with Mac. But I haven't gotten up this way much in the past two or three years, except for the company retreats." She started stacking the twigs and branches on top of the bed of birch bark. "I thought it was time I did the sophisticated Europe and Caribbean tours, and Mac encouraged me to go. He said it was good for me to broaden my horizons, so I did. Alison and I went together."

Nick remembered that Alison was Tracy's sister. Somehow he'd always had the notion that the two girls weren't close, probably because Alison, not involved in Sunstone, rarely was around. "And how were Europe and the Caribbean with Alison?" he asked casually, carrying the firewood over to the rock and putting it down beside Tracy.

"Great," she said with a smile. "The wood, I mean. But so were the trips. Alison and I had a lot of fun together. The thing is, she never took to the bush the way I did, and she'd always wanted to work in Mom's chain of fashion boutiques, so we'd gone in different directions over the years. Down in the relaxed atmosphere of the tropics we reverted to our adolescence, sitting up half the night giggling, doing each other's hair, playing with makeup. Girl stuff, you know? Europe was nice in a different way. Alison's the artistic one and I'm a history nut, so I had a personal tour guide for the galleries and shops, and she had one for the museums and graveyards." Getting to her feet, Tracy wiped her hands on the back of her jeans. "Alison and I are as different as my mother and my grandfather, so we complement each other pretty well."

Nick found the picture of the two girls endearing. It was obvious he'd been wrong on yet another score: they were close. He couldn't figure it. Wasn't he supposed to be such a canny judge of people? Why the blind spot for Tracy?

It wasn't really such a puzzle, he conceded. After all, he'd told himself, a Tracy Carlisle who was a spoiled, coldhearted little princess wasn't his type. His pride had been protected too. Nick Corcoran would never woo the boss's granddaughter, no sir-ree. That was the cheap way to get to the top. So it followed he'd believed he mustn't take a chance on falling for her. There were too many complications. Suddenly something she'd said came back to him. "Graveyards?" he repeated.

She'd taken her emergency kit from the duffel bag and was opening the container of wooden matches. "I like old graveyards," she said with a smile. "It's a different kind of history than you get from books. More of a living thing . . ." She realized the phrase was ill chosen. "Well, not exactly *living*, I guess. But real. Sort of . . . personal." She realized she was chattering aimlessly, something she never did with anyone outside her immediate family. "Alison says I'm weird," she finished lamely.

"Alison is right," Nick said, ruffling her hair. He went to the balsam tree to cut the branches for their bed, not minding the chore at all.

Tracy struck a match and held it under the curls of birch bark. They caught fire instantly, and soon the kindling was burning with a pungent scent that Nick found more heady than any perfume.

In no time the campfire was blazing while the beans heated in one pot and water boiled for tea in another. Tracy was stirring up the sourdough mix she'd found in one of Red's survival-food envelopes, and Nick was spreading out balsam branches under an evergreen that Tracy assured him was protection enough from the rain, which had slowed to a light drizzle. But the sky was turning black as low rumblings sounded in the distance, and Nick looked up just as the tiresome plane overhead stopped its futile search and started away.

"Look," he said. "It seems our airborne bloodhound is finally giving up the hunt."

Tracy watched the direction of the plane's flight and relief washed over her with such force, she had to admit to herself for the first time how afraid she'd been all afternoon. "Walt's going north," she said, exulting in the implication of Cooper's choice. "He isn't heading for Sunstone Lake. He's going back to the cabin. So you're right, Nick. He hasn't admitted to Mac that he's lost us." Her voice dropped almost to a whisper. "Mac is safe, at least for tonight." She was silent for a moment, then spoke gravely. "I have no idea whether Walt actually hoped to spot us or was just playing at psychological warfare, but either way he knows now what a waste his efforts today have been. He'll try something else tomorrow. It doesn't matter. It just doesn't matter what he tries. His stupid game is over whether he realizes it or not."

Nick heard more determination than conviction in Tracy's words, yet he believed her. Walt Cooper had been beaten before he'd begun. The man had chosen the wrong victim when he'd picked on fragile little Tracy Carlisle.

With the droning aircraft gone, the forest seemed eerily still. Nick felt as if he and Tracy were the only two people left in the world, and in a way it was a pleasant sensation. Apart from his desire to get to Mac and tell him all was well, he found he wasn't eager to return to civilization.

He was getting ahead of himself. He and Tracy were a long way from making it back to their normal world, with no guarantees they ever would. Who knew what Cooper might try next? At worst, he could do what Tracy feared most: make her grandfather the prisoner and demand ransom for him. In fact, there was something puzzling about the fact that Mac hadn't been the chosen victim in the first place.

Another question nagged at Nick. How had Walt Cooper known exactly what kind of plane was expected to pick Tracy up and at exactly what time?

Only a few people had been privy to that information. A few of Sunstone's top executives.

A deep anger gripped Nick—and another emotion he couldn't quite peg. An emotion so foreign to him yet so powerful, he knew it was going to change irrevocably his entire existence. His very being.

"How's this?" he asked Tracy, his voice strained as he smiled and indicated his handmade mattress.

Tracy looked at the bed she would share with him later and felt strangely contented, mysteriously confident of the future. "Perfect," she said softly. "Nothing could be more perfect."

Six

"I never knew beans and sourdough bread could taste so good," Nick remarked, carrying the dishes to the stream to wash them.

Tracy smiled and bent to fish her small flashlight from the duffel bag. "It's really getting dark," she said, taking the light over to Nick. "Especially away from the fire." Returning to the bag, she found the ground sheet in her emergency kit and began unfolding it. "You know, I hated beans when I was little until Mac conned me into liking them," she reminisced aloud, still feeling better about her grandfather, convinced he was in no trouble yet.

Nick wedged the light between two rocks and began using sand from the stream bed to scrub the plates and utensils. "How did Mac con you into liking beans?" he asked, though he'd always suspected Mac could con anyone into anything.

"Simple," Tracy said, smiling fondly as she recalled one of the many good times she'd had with her grandfather in this very forest. "He told me real woodsmen loved beans. I wanted to be a real woodsman, so . . ."

"That was all it took?" Nick asked with a chuckle.

"I'm afraid I was very impressionable," Tracy admitted. "But the big test was when Mac was in too much of a hurry one day to build a fire and beans were on the menu." Tracy spread the ground sheet over the balsam boughs and began smoothing it. "I drew the line at *cold* beans. Yucky, I believe I called them. Yucky and gross."

Rinsing the dishes under a miniature waterfall, Nick conjured up a mental picture of Tracy turning up her pert nose at a plate of cold beans. He found himself wishing he'd known that little girl. "Who won the day? You or Mac?"

"Mac, of course," Tracy said with a quiet laugh. "He always did, you know." She paused, looking off into the distance. "Always does, always will," she added softly before going on. "He gave me the usual line about how real woodsmen depended on beans, hot or cold, because it made them strong. He said every real woodsman knew that the secret of Paul Bunyan's power was that he ate his beans right from the can."

"Like Popeye and spinach," Nick commented, grinning.

"Exactly. But I didn't think I wanted to be a real woodsman *that* badly, and I was beginning to entertain doubts about Paul Bunyan, having just learned the sad truth about Santa Claus, so I wasn't buying his story. Well, Mac went over to a maple tree—not just any maple, mind you, but Moose maple—and snapped off a couple of leaves. The leaves were the size of plates. He put them on a log and told me to guard them so they wouldn't blow away. While I stood guard, Mac whittled two flat sticks, handed one to me, put a helping of beans in the center of each leaf, and told me that he was letting me in on a very special secret of northern woodsmen. If I took just one taste, he said, I'd know why it was such a well-kept secret, because the two magic ingredients were the moose maple leaf for a plate and the freshly cut wood for a spoon. Any other combination just didn't have that special flavor and certainly wouldn't make anyone strong. By the time he'd started eating his beans he had me. I ate my beans—cold—and loved them."

"Did you become strong?" Nick asked, his voice husky with emotion as this chatterbox of a woman utterly enchanted him.

"*I* thought so. I went around flexing my biceps, absolutely convinced they were getting bigger and harder by the hour."

"Gullible little thing, weren't you?" Nick teased. "How long ago was all this?"

"About a year ago," Tracy shot back, her lips quirking with a suppressed grin.

Nick did a double take, then laughed and felt a surge of affection that was so strong, it shook him up a little. "You're a real brat, Tracy Carlisle. Was that whole story a setup?"

Tracy laughed with him, then put up her hand in a scout's-honor gesture. "Every word was true, except that I think I was about eight when Mac did the cold-beans number on me." All at once she realized how easy it was to talk to Nick, even kid with him. She'd never imagined she could relax with him so completely. With anyone, in fact, outside her family. And the expression in his eyes as he looked at her . . .

She cleared her throat, hating herself for breaking the spell between them but too new at being happy with Nick to know just how to handle it. "I'll see what else is in our little bag of tricks," she said with a nervous smile. Dropping to a crouch, she took out the toiletry pouch she'd tossed into the backpack at the last minute. Opening the kit, she began taking things out. "Hey, great," she said, feeling herself beginning to chatter nervously. "I'd forgotten just what was in here. Lots of goodies. Toothbrushes, and, let's see . . . a couple of little bars of soap . . ." She rummaged in the bag, taking out a lipstick-size deodorant stick, a couple of travel envelopes of shampoo, and a packet of tissues. "All the comforts of home," she said at last, then clamped her mouth shut before she could entertain Nick with any more of her mindless drivel.

Nick got a kick out of the fact that even in the midst of escaping through a northern wilderness, Tracy Carlisle observed the niceties.

They finished their chores and retired to separate areas to freshen up. Nick was tense the whole time Tracy was out of his sight. "You weren't nervous about wild animals?" he asked when she finally got back and he could breathe easily again.

Tracy ruffled her fingers through her hair to dry the damp strands. "Wild animals?" she repeated. "The only ones that worry me are the two-legged kind, and they're probably getting drunk back in their filthy old shack."

"What about bears?" Nick asked, wondering if they

should take some precautions. "I'm no camper, but I've heard tales of attacks happening right in national parks."

"They happen because people are dumb enough to leave food and garbage lying around. The bears are naturally attracted, get all upset and scared when the screaming starts, and then the poor animals take the rap for the so-called attack. We've been careful, so unless there's some renegade bear running around dependent on stealing from people and rooting through garbage dumps, we can be sure the creatures of this forest prefer to give us a wide berth."

"Unless there's some renegade bear," Nick said dryly, resting his hands on his hips and trying not to grin. "Comforting, Tracy. You can't imagine how much safer I feel since you explained that to me."

She laughed. "I hardly think we need to worry in this area. We're miles and miles from garbage dumps and other earmarks of civilization. Besides, Mac told me what to do when suddenly confronted by a bear."

"And just what would that be?" Nick asked with exaggerated interest.

Tracy treated the question seriously. "Well, whatever you do, don't run. Don't make any sudden moves at all. And never, never climb a tree. Just stay calm and walk backward, very slowly."

"Walk backward," Nick repeated.

"Right. Slowly, though."

Nodding, Nick considered that bit of information. "Walk backward to where, Tracy?"

She stared at him for several seconds, then shrugged nonchalantly. "You know, it never occurred to me to ask!"

Nick lunged for her, but she darted out of his

reach. "I'm serious!" she protested as he gave her a dangerous look. "I really never thought to ask! Mac said walk backward, so I just figured if the occasion ever arose, I'd do that for a few steps and the bear would go away. Honestly, I wasn't putting you on!"

"Maybe not *that* time," Nick conceded. "But I'm gaining a healthy wariness about anything you tell me, sweetheart." He looked around the campsite. "You say we've been careful enough not to attract bears. Are there any more little housekeeping jobs that need to be done before we turn in?" Though he tried to sound casual, he felt his throat tightening on the last words. It seemed so natural to talk to Tracy as if "turning in" were something they did together every night.

Tracy couldn't answer at first. Her pulse had started throbbing a primitive, giddy rhythm. The power of speech had temporarily deserted her.

Finally she fastened her attention on the duffel bag. "You know, if we take out everything hard from that bag and put in your jacket and my sweatshirt, we'll have a pillow. We can stuff balsam boughs into the sleeping bag carrier for another one."

"Good idea," Nick agreed, starting right away to gather loose boughs. "You know, you were right a while ago. We have all the comforts of home—thanks to your ingenuity and that magician's hat of supplies you put together."

Tracy laughed quietly as she unrolled the sleeping bag. "Now you know why the backpack was so heavy."

"The cans of beans were the only real weight," Nick reminded her, quickly making the balsam pillow. "I'm amazed how much you managed to pack and at how much you lifted from the cabin in such a short time. Even a can opener, for Pete's sake. And tea bags. You cased the joint and then cleaned it out like a pro." Disgustedly he added, "Meanwhile I was getting myself trussed up like a turkey."

"You had no choice," Tracy shot back, instantly springing to his defense. "I know perfectly well that if you'd been alone, you'd have fought back, but you wouldn't take the chance because of me." With an eloquent snap of her wrists she tossed the sleeping bag over the ground sheet.

Nick put the makeshift pillow in place, then slowly approached Tracy, grinning. "You get pretty ferocious when you're defending someone you care about."

Tracy felt excitement rising within her as Nick drew near in the enveloping darkness, the flickering light from their waning campfire playing over his strong features.

He took another step toward her. "You care about me, Tracy," he stated softly. "You've cared about me for a long time." He reached for her, spanning her waist with his hands. "How long, sweetheart? Exactly how many weeks or months or years have I been a blind idiot?"

Placing her hands on his chest, she felt his racing heartbeat against her palms and knew he wasn't as calm as he was trying to appear. That small evidence of his vulnerability gave her the courage to speak the truth. "About three," she told him in a small voice. "I mean, not that you've been a blind idiot . . . just that I . . . ."

"Three what?" he asked, pulling her closer until their bodies were touching, his hands still on her waist, his lips grazing gentle kisses over her up-turned face. "Three weeks? Months?"

"Years," Tracy said as a shiver of pleasure rippled through her. "Remember that first time Mac brought you home to dinner? Before you'd even accepted the position he'd offered you? Right away I . . . I knew that . . . that you were very special," she said, suddenly nervous again, afraid she was confessing too much. "And you *are* special, Nick. My goodness, I can't imagine what my grandfather would do without you. Especially since Roy Harlan died and Mac felt he had to appoint Hugh in his father's place and all those retirements of Mac's old cronies meant he had to deal with a bunch of new faces, men with more ambition than experience, and they don't have the same sense of loyalty Mac had always counted on, except you, of course—"

Nick's mouth found hers and effectively stopped her compulsive chatter, his tongue taking full advantage of her parted lips, surprising and thrilling her with its bold, demanding thrusts. He moved his hands over her back, molding her to him, while she inched her fingers upward to dig into his shoulders, clinging for support as her body was drained of its strength. Heat poured into her from Nick's hands and pervaded every part of her. With her breasts swelling against the solid wall of his chest, her hips moving instinctively to fit themselves to his, she arched into the pulsating, hard warmth of him.

Nick released her mouth and raised his head slightly to gaze down at her in wonder. Never in his life had he experienced such desire, a need that threatened to override all rational considerations in its compulsion to be fulfilled. "Tracy, sweetheart," he said in a near whisper. "I don't know what's happening here. I want you more than I ever knew I could want anyone. But a part of me is . . . I'm not sure I trust . . ." He trailed off too confused to sort out the thoughts and feelings gripping him. All he knew for certain was that this day had changed everything, turned his whole life upside down.

Tracy saw the confusion in his eyes and understood just what Nick was going through. But she didn't care what happened tomorrow or the day after that; she wouldn't be cheated of loving Nick, if only for a few hours. Touching her fingers to his lips, she smiled. "I want you too, Nick. So much. No strings, no promises, no complications."

Nick was troubled by her words. Yet weren't they exactly what he wanted to hear? "Maybe I want strings and promises and complications," he said, surprising himself. "Maybe I want more with you than just tonight."

"But we won't know that until we've left these strange circumstances behind," Tracy reminded him. "And I don't know about you, but I don't want to wait. I've waited long enough, Nick." Deciding that his scruples were best forgotten for a while, she took the initiative, standing on tiptoe to steal a kiss. Seductively she ran her tongue along the inside of his lips, circling his mouth. "It's astonishing," she said, then paused to dip her tongue into the minty sweetness again. Tilting back her head and closing her eyes, she savored the delicious nectar like a connoisseur with a rare wine. "Just astonishing," she repeated. "In your mouth even that awful-tasting toothpaste is transformed into ambrosia. I believe I'd like some more." With Nick's surprised, low chuckle vibrating against her lips and her hands fanned behind his head, she delved her tongue into his mouth.

Nick's mind whirled and all his senses careened out of control. Tracy's sweet aggressiveness obliterated every doubt and unleashed the driving hunger that had been gnawing at him. "Sweetheart," he said in a half groan when she released his mouth and he could brush his lips over the delicate column of her throat. There was so much he wanted to tell her: How her skin delighted him, so silky and cool and fresh; how her gentle feminine curves intrigued him; how her eyes had haunted him even when he'd battled their hypnotic effects.

But every part of his body was surging, pounding, thrusting with a primitive power. He hardly was aware of pulling Tracy's two shirts over her head, one after the other in quick succession, of removing her bra, then shedding his own jacket and shirt so he could feel her against him. In the faint glow that remained from the fire's embers, she gleamed like an alabaster sculpture, pale and perfect, but her body was alive, warm, soft. Nick smoothed his palms over every inch of her naked torso, then bent his head to her breasts, swirling his tongue around each velvety pink tip, tasting tiny drops of rain that had filtered through the leafy canopy. As his hands cupped and kneaded her high, firm mounds, he lost himself in all her textures and reveled in her sharp gasps of pleasure. The same atavistic male power that had coursed wildly through him moments earlier suddenly gave him the strength to be patient. His caresses became slow and measured as he found countless ways to please Tracy—and himself.

For Tracy it was an exquisite torment she wished would never end. Nick sucked at her breasts, his hands stroking her back and shoulders and arms. He raised his head and toyed with her mouth, nibbling at her lower lip, inviting her tongue to dance with his. He held her so the tips of her breasts, now excruciatingly sensitive, whispered over the thatch of hair on his chest. Then, without warning, he crushed her against him, his arms imprisoning her while he possessed her mouth, his tongue plunging rhythmically in and out in a perfect mime of the deeper union to follow.

Finally lifting his head again, Nick showered kisses over Tracy's face, licking the balsam-scented mist from her cheeks and trailing the tip of his tongue downward over her throat, the pulse spot at its base, the cleft between her breasts. As he dropped to one knee he smiled up at her and proceeded to remove her shoes and socks, occasionally touching his lips to her midriff or her breasts as he worked.

Tracy smiled dreamily and realized she was in just the right position to indulge her fantasy of tousling Nick's hair, of raking her fingers through the silky chestnut strands, of stroking the nape of his neck as his quiet sigh told her he liked the gesture very much. "Now I *know* you're very special," she murmured. "It takes a special man to make a romantic moment of removing a lady's sneakers."

"It takes a special lady," he replied as his hands went to the fastening of her jeans, "to inspire him to such romantic moments." Slowly, patiently, he peeled off her jeans. "Man-styled bikinis," he remarked when they were all she was wearing, then grazed his lips along the outline of the briefs—the low waist, the curve of each thigh. "I'll bet they've never looked so feminine," he added as his tongue followed the same path.

Tracy began trembling. She'd wanted Nick before he'd ever touched her. Now the intensity of her desire was almost unbearable.

He tugged off her briefs, then remained where he was for a moment just gazing at her, awed by her loveliness.

Tracy clutched at his shoulders as a spasm of need racked her body. "Nick . . . dear heaven. Nick . . ."

He stood up. "Are you cold, sweetheart?" he asked as he lifted her into his arms and carefully placed her on top of their bed, then lay beside her and cradled her with a protectiveness that brought tears to her eyes. "I'll warm you, love," he said, drawing the sleeping bag around her.

Though Tracy wasn't at all cold, she liked Nick's cuddling too much to protest, so she nuzzled her face happily into the warm, fragrant hollow of his neck. But somehow her hand crept downward to his belt buckle and began struggling to unfasten it.

Laughing quietly, Nick sat up long enough to divest himself of his clothes, then stretched out again beside Tracy. "*Now* I'll warm you," he said in a mock growl, adding in a gentler tone, "and myself too."

But he was wrong. It was Tracy who warmed him. She responded to his caresses with a fire that consumed him. Not satisfied to be explored and teased and tasted, she did her own exploring and teasing and tasting, learning the planes and hollows of his body as he learned hers.

At last Nick knew he couldn't hold back any longer.

And as Tracy wrapped her legs around him to urge him into her, he knew she couldn't wait another moment either. The expression of bliss he saw in her glazed eyes as he filled her with himself was as exciting as the way her moist warmth surrounded and gripped him. As he watched Tracy's face, seeing a pink flush spread over her breasts and throat, the unfamiliar feeling he'd been unable or unwilling to identify began gathering force until it was carrying him along on its current—and Tracy with him. They entered a new dimension, where time was measured only by their entwined rhythm and space was limited to their private, fragrant bedchamber. Nick had stopped trying to control anything, to do anything but flow with Tracy toward the precipice ahead.

They reached the abyss. Nick enfolded Tracy in his arms, and she clung to him as they were swept over the edge. Their muffled cries blended with the other muted sounds of the forest—the loons calling to one another, the rustle of damp leaves as rain washed over them, the gurgling of the stream as it spilled down the hillside.

Nick held Tracy until the rain and the night's cool breeze made him stir, regretfully. "I guess we should put on some clothes and get under this sleeping bag," he said, his lips close to her ear.

"I suppose so," Tracy agreed with a sigh. She tipped back her head and kissed the underside of Nick's chin. "Now I know what it must feel like to go over Niagara Falls."

Nick hugged her. "And without a barrel at that."

"You were my barrel, Nick," she said seriously.

"And you were mine," he told her, then chuckled.

"Does it also take a special pair of people to call each other barrels and consider it romantic?"

"Definitely special people," Tracy said, laughing with him.

They made themselves do the practical thing and were under the sleeping bag, fully dressed, when the last orange-red ember of their fire died.

They were both asleep within minutes.

Seven

When Tracy opened her eyes to the dawn mist, she felt it seeping into her spirit, filling her with a cold dread.

Even as a child she'd always loved the first veiled light of morning in the forest and often had imagined herself in an enchanted wood where any magical adventure might come her way.

But the fog that had descended around her now was chilling and oppressive, an ectoplasm teeming with her deepest fears.

She shivered, and even in his sleep Nick instinctively tucked her closer to him as his body pressed against her back, spoon-style. A moment later he stirred, then whispered close to her ear, "You're awake?"

Tracy turned so she was lying on her back, Nick's arm, warm and heavy and reassuring, over her waist. "How do you feel?" she asked. "Many aches and pains?"

"I'm not sure. I'll let you know when I try to get up. But I slept . . ." He lifted his arm from Tracy as he covered a yawn. "Boy, did I sleep. You?"

"Never better," she said honestly. But she wondered why all her confidence had fled this morning. She wasn't sure any longer of Mac's safety, and suddenly she wasn't so cocky about her ability to handle her feelings for Nick. She had no regrets about the previous night, but just as she'd anticipated, making love with him had profoundly affected her—and would change a lot of things in her life. From now on Nick would know her as no one else ever had. From now on she couldn't pretend cool indifference even if the time came when she'd need to.

She wondered what Nick was feeling. For her their loving had been too poignantly sweet to toss off lightly. For him? She wasn't sure. "Are you hungry?" she asked, her voice strained as she made a move to get up.

Nick didn't release her. "Depends what we've got," he said sleepily. "I noticed an envelope of dehydrated chicken chow mein. I don't think I'm *that* hungry." What he *was* hungry for, he realized bemusedly, was Tracy. Only Tracy. But the morning was cold and damp, and reality couldn't be set aside even for a little while. They had to keep pushing ahead. There was time enough for pleasure later. Nevertheless, he refused to let Tracy budge for another few minutes, snuggling her against him as they shared each other's warmth.

Her body felt tense, he noticed. It didn't take much to understand why. Not only were her fears for Mac flooding back, she obviously was suffering from a morning-after affliction more painful than the worst hangover: a fear that she'd given herself too completely, made herself too vulnerable. Nick remembered that unpleasant rush of self-doubt all too well, though he'd experienced it only once and very long ago.

He tried to reassure Tracy. "Nothing's different this morning, love," he said. "We're still okay and so is Mac. And last night . . . well, last night was—" He paused, swallowing hard as emotion welled up in him. There were no adequate words.

"You don't have to say anything," Tracy said hastily. "No strings, remember? No complications."

Nick was about to remind her that he'd suggested he might want strings and complications when it occurred to him he was being pretty presumptuous. Obviously Tracy cared for him, but was she making promises or stating terms? Was Tracy the one who wanted to keep their lovemaking uncomplicated? Was she the one who couldn't set aside their rivalry, who didn't want him to get the wrong idea about her intentions?

He realized his ego might have led him astray. He'd started thinking about how the two of them could transcend the complications, but it seemed that Tracy just wanted to deny them. "So what *do* we have for breakfast?" he asked lightly, releasing her.

"Trail mix," she said as she sat up, trying to battle her disappointment. When she made a promise, she meant it. No strings. Yet she couldn't help wishing . . . "I'm going to take one of my private little walks," she announced, getting to her feet. Her muscles ached a bit but not enough to make her admit it. "Be back in a minute," she added, grabbing her toothbrush and other toiletries before she hurried away.

"Want me to build a fire for tea?" Nick called after her, hurt by her sudden coolness but determined not to show it. He'd done that once, almost a decade ago, and he'd ended up looking like a fool. "Don't read so much into last night's bit of fun," Christina Jansen had told him with the throaty laugh that had attracted him to her in the first place. "Don't spoil everything by turning all *serious* on me, darling. Besides, we do have to work together, remember? We must maintain a certain . . . decorum." The steamy night she'd shared with Nick Corcoran hadn't deterred Christina in the least from stabbing him in the back to beat him to a promotion. She'd been an early, effective teacher in the art of corporate and romantic survival.

Never again, Nick had decided then. And he wouldn't back down now. Not even for Tracy. "What about it?" he asked. "A fire?"

Tracy hadn't been able to answer Nick at first, an annoying and childish lump filling her throat just because he'd let her go so easily. What had she expected? After three years of practically hating her, was he going to do a complete about-face because of a few romantic hours in the dark? She swallowed hard. "If you want tea, go ahead with the fire," she called over her shoulder. "It doesn't matter to me. Plain water would be fine. But the sooner we start traveling, the better."

Nick shrugged and decided against a fire. Tracy was right. They had to make tracks. But his stomach knotted with sudden tension as she disappeared into the gray mist. What had happened to their closeness?

Tracy went down to the lake to wash up, crouching on a rock that sloped into the water. Belatedly she remembered Nick's tenderness, his patient love-making, the laughter they'd shared. She recalled how he'd flung himself over her when he'd thought someone was shooting at them.

How dishonest of her, she thought. She'd promised love without complications and delivered petulance at the first test.

She wanted to make it up to him somehow. After a casual glance around the shoreline, she came up with an idea.

Nick was beginning to pace. Reluctant to intrude on her privacy, he didn't want to go after Tracy, but she'd been gone too long. He'd already freshened up, dug out the trail mix, packed up the sleeping bag, and still she hadn't come back. Wild fears began taking hold in Nick's imagination: Renegade bears, kidnappers with unexpected tracking skills, wolves . . . "Dammit, Tracy!" he exploded when she finally wandered back to the campsite. "Where the hell were you?"

She stopped and stared at him, her eyes huge. "Just down at the lake," she said softly, thrilled by his obvious agitation. Had he been that worried about her? She held up her peace offering. "Getting these for our breakfast. I thought they might make the trail mix more palatable."

Nick looked down and in the next second was back in the grip of the feelings that had swept over him the night before when Tracy was in his arms. "Where did that basket come from?" he asked, his voice thick with emotion.

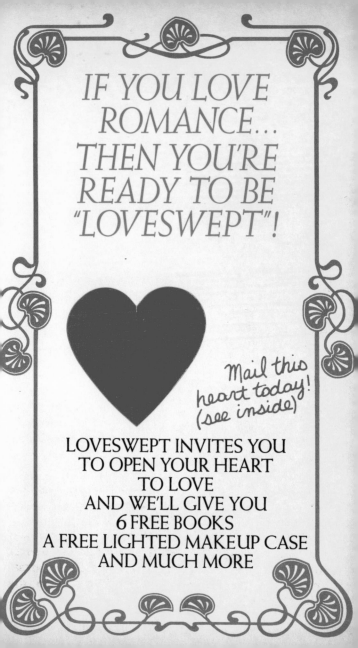

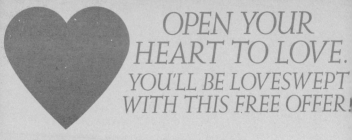

OPEN YOUR HEART TO LOVE. YOU'LL BE LOVESWEPT WITH THIS FREE OFFER!

HERE'S WHAT YOU GET:

1. **FREE!** SIX NEW LOVESWEPT NOVELS! You get 6 beautiful stories filled with passion, romance, laughter, and tears... exciting romances to stir the excitement of falling in love... again and again.

2. **FREE!** A BEAUTIFUL MAKEUP CASE WITH A MIRROR THAT LIGHTS UP! What could be more useful than a makeup case with a mirror that lights up*? Once you open the tortoise-shell finish case, you have a choice of brushes... for your lips, your eyes, and your blushing cheeks.

*(batteries not included)

3. **SAVE!** MONEY-SAVING HOME DELIVERY! Join the Loveswept at-home reader service and we'll send you 6 new novels each month. You always get 15 days to preview them before you decide. Each book is yours for only $2.09 — a savings of 41¢ per book.

4. **BEAT THE CROWDS!** You'll always receive your Loveswept books before they are available in bookstores. You'll be the first to thrill to these exciting new stories.

BE LOVESWEPT TODAY — JUST COMPLETE, DETACH AND MAIL YOUR FREE-OFFER CARD.

FREE-LIGHTED MAKEUP CASE!
FREE-6 LOVESWEPT NOVELS!

- NO OBLIGATION
- NO PURCHASE NECESSARY

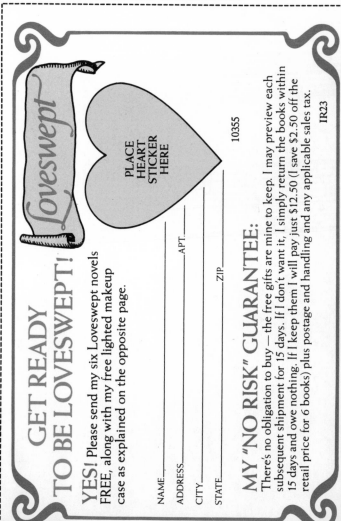

GET READY TO BE LOVESWEPT!

YES! Please send my six Loveswept novels FREE, along with my free lighted makeup case as explained on the opposite page.

PLACE HEART STICKER HERE

10355

NAME _____

ADDRESS _____ APT. ____

CITY _____

STATE _____ ZIP _____

MY "NO RISK" GUARANTEE:

There's no obligation to buy — the free gifts are mine to keep. I may preview each subsequent shipment for 15 days. If I don't want it, I simply return the books within 15 days and owe nothing. If I keep them I will pay just $12.50 (I save $2.50 off the retail price for 6 books) plus postage and handling and any applicable sales tax.

IR23

REMEMBER!

- The free books and gift are mine to keep!
- There is no obligation!
- I may preview each shipment for 15 days!
- I can cancel anytime!

BUSINESS REPLY MAIL

FIRST-CLASS MAIL   PERMIT NO. 2456   HICKSVILLE, N.Y.

POSTAGE WILL BE PAID BY ADDRESSEE

Loveswept

Bantam Books
P.O. Box 985
Hicksville, NY 11802-9827

NO POSTAGE
NECESSARY
IF MAILED
IN THE
UNITED STATES

"I made it," Tracy explained with a faint smile as she tried to read the strange expression in Nick's eyes. "To carry the blueberries. I can't pick berries without eating them, so I've had my fill. These are for you. Sort of a present. A little surprise."

Nick smiled as he accepted the gift, though there was an embarrassing hint of moisture in his eyes. "You made a basket with birch bark and—" He examined her handiwork. "And twigs for staples. And you filled it with blueberries as a surprise for me."

"You do like wild blueberries?" Tracy asked eagerly. "These are wonderful. Sweet and juicy and right at the peak of ripeness."

Nick tasted one, then another. "Beautiful," he said, his gaze holding Tracy's. "Sweet and juicy and right at the peak of ripeness." He couldn't resist. "And the berries ain't bad either."

Though Tracy laughed, she felt a flush stealing over her cheeks. Nick's teasing remark brought back a rush of memories of the unbelievable intimacy she'd shared with him. Looking around the campsite, she raised her brows. "I see you've been busy. We're just about set to go."

"As soon as we've stoked up on trail mix," Nick said, putting his arm around Tracy's shoulders, feeling very close to her again and liking the sensation. He guided her to the rock where he'd left a cup of water and the envelopes of the dried fruit and nuts. Sitting down beside her, he put the basket of berries between them. "Have some of these, honey."

"But I told you—"

"Have some," Nick insisted. "At least enough to sparkle up this bird seed."

"You're not a fan of trail mix, I gather," Tracy said

with a grin as she accepted a few berries and dropped them into her envelope of raisins, oatmeal, cashews, and almonds.

Nick tossed some almonds into his mouth. "Since it stands between us and starvation," he said a moment later, "I'm nuts about the stuff."

Tracy wasn't about to let that one go by. "Nuts about it? And you make derogatory comments about *my* puns?"

Nick chuckled, remembering her courageous silliness the previous day. "But mine was innocent. Yours are premeditated."

The fog was lifting slowly and with it Tracy's mood. "You know, we might manage to reach the tracks in time to catch the late afternoon eastbound train," she remarked before popping a handful of trail mix into her mouth.

Nick gave her a surprised look. "You've memorized the schedules? Or are you going to tell me you've even got one of those in your emergency kit?"

"I haven't," Tracy answered, laughing. "But Mac gets some of his supplies by train. One of the nice things about this part of the country is that a lot of things stay the same year after year—including the railroad schedules."

"Still, how do you happen to remember them?" Nick asked, aware that Tracy hadn't spent much time at Mac's forest retreat in the past few years.

"When I was a kid staying at the lodge for a couple of weeks at a time, we'd take Mac's little motorboat across Sunstone Lake, then portage to the tracks and flag down the local just to send out some mail."

Nick looked at her with a dubious expression. "You're going to tell me the train would stop and the engineer would lean out to catch the letters you tossed to him, right?"

"It didn't stop," she said blithely. "Just slowed down. And it wasn't the engineer who took the letters. It was the man in the mail car. He'd stand in the open doorway—"

"Tracy, is this one of your put-ons?" Nick interrupted. "Because if it is . . ."

"It's the absolute gospel, Nick! Why are you so suspicious? Would I kid you?"

"I wish I knew," he said, grumbling, feigning gruffness. "I'll just have to check you out with your grandfather."

Tracy tipped back her head and laughed heartily.

Nick got to his feet and stood in front of her, placing his hands on either side of her body and leaning down so his face was very close to hers. "I said something funny?"

"You'll check *me* out with *Mac*? Has he ever got *you* fooled, Nick Corcoran!"

Nick's scowl wasn't entirely a pretense by this time. "Bill MacKay is the most honest man I've ever known," he stated just a bit hesitantly.

"Oh, he's honest when it comes to anything that counts," Tracy explained, her blue eyes filled with merriment as she looked up at Nick.

He wished he could hold on to the moment forever.

"But my grandfather can't be trusted for a second," Tracy continued. "Not when he decides to have a little fun. He's had me tramping through the thickest, nastiest bush over the worst terrain and doing it eagerly because we were looking for the UFO he still insists he saw crash somewhere near Sunstone Lake. He's sent me to fetch left-handed nails, a hundred yards of shoreline, a can of elbow grease . . ."

"You didn't fall for those old clinkers," Nick chided, undecided whether to kiss her or let her keep talking, while he lost himself in the endless blue of her eyes. "Tell me you weren't that easy a mark."

"I'm afraid I was," Tracy admitted readily. "And you would be, too, if Mac ever decided to pick on you. He's very convincing, you know. I'm still not sure whether or not the big forest fire up here in 1948 sent up such a cloud of smoke it blanketed Scotland for a month."

"We could look it up," Nick suggested, trying to decide whether he dared kiss Tracy. Would he be able to stop at just a kiss? "That's something we could check out," he added softly.

Tracy felt a buzzing along her spine as Nick's voice deepened, his eyes darkening to a smoky green. "That wouldn't be any fun," she argued absently, her mind no longer on tall tales. "You just have to decide whether to believe or not."

"Maybe it's always better to believe," he said, the decision made for him by the irresistible invitation of Tracy's full, parted lips.

His mouth touched hers, the contact so light and sweet that when he drew back, Tracy leaned forward, reluctant to let him go.

Nick took a deep breath and smiled at her. "That was a mistake I couldn't help making. Now I'll pay for it by wanting you even more than I did before."

Tracy bit down on her lower lip. "Ditto," she whispered, knowing they had to get back on the trail. All temptation to linger and make love was banished by the thought of Mac alone at the lodge while Walt Cooper revised his original plans.

Nick straightened up, drained the cup of water,

and dipped more from the stream. "We'll have to go around that lake," he said as he handed the cup to Tracy. "Isn't it going to be tough to use landmarks to keep track of our direction? The sky's still pretty overcast, so we can't even see where the sun is. Any ideas?"

Tracy studied the sky. "Sure wish I had a piece of sunstone," she said.

Kneeling to pack the cup away, Nick frowned up at Tracy, wondering what she was talking about. Why would she talk business at a time like this? Was that where her thoughts were after all? "But you do have a piece of Sunstone," he commented, picking up the backpack and starting to slide his arms through the straps. "You have shares in the company."

Tracy touched his shoulder. "Before you put that on your back I need one more thing from the emergency kit."

Nick put the bag down, still perplexed by Tracy's remark. "And Mac makes no secret about the fact that you'll inherit more shares eventually, perhaps all of his."

Tracy realized what she'd said and what Nick had naturally assumed she meant. "I was speaking geologically," she said, frowning as she searched for the kit. Any mention of her inheritance was upsetting. The only thing she was interested in was Mac himself. She wanted him to live forever. If that couldn't be arranged, she at least wanted many more years with him. At this point she wasn't sure he'd make it through the day. Swallowing hard, she battled a rising tide of fear. "By sunstone," she told him, her mind only half on what she was saying, "I meant a rock. I wish I had a sample now. Mac told me how Norsemen apparently used a crystalline rock to locate the sun on an overcast day. They would hold up the rock and move it around, watching a mark they'd put on it, I suppose, on a day when they could see the sun. As soon as that point took on a special translucence, they knew they'd located the sun because that was where the rays were hitting most directly. Nick, we *have* to get to my grandfather! We *can't* let Walt Cooper hurt him or hold him for ransom!" She covered her face with her hands.

Nick almost had seen the pattern of Tracy's thoughts, and he felt like kicking himself for his stupid remark about her inheritance. Dropping to his knees, he dragged her into his arms and stroked her hair. "We'll get there, honey. We will. And you know how strong Mac is. How canny. He'll have Walt Cooper running around in circles trying to figure out where everything went wrong. You know that, Tracy. Cooper's no match for Bill MacKay, is he?"

Lowering her hands, Tracy shook her head. "No, of course not," she managed to answer.

"Now, what were you looking for? Your emergency kit?" Nick asked. He cradled her face in his hands and kissed her eyelids.

Tracy nodded. "I guess I was too busy yakking and fussing to find anything in the backpack. I couldn't think."

Nick grinned and chucked her under the chin, then found the kit, handed it to her, and got to his feet. "I'm not surprised you couldn't think," he said teasingly. "Not with that balderdash you were trying to give me about sunstones, Norsemen . . ."

"It was all true," Tracy protested, smiling again

and remembering what she'd wanted from the kit. She'd planned to have a little fun at Nick's expense. But he was being so dear, so gentle.

Nick rolled his eyes in disbelief. "You do try a man's patience, Miss Carlisle."

"You have a real problem with trust, you know that?" Tracy stated, deciding to go through with her plan. Casually turning away from him, she opened the kit and pocketed one item from it, then returned it to the duffel bag.

"You can't even face me with this one," he insisted, deliberately trying to provoke her. A feisty Tracy was able to rise above her fear. "You're a real brat, Tracy Carlisle. These yarns just spin out of you."

"I told you the truth," Tracy insisted, getting frustrated with his doubts, though she didn't really blame him. "Honestly, Nick. I *did!*"

"Then you're repeating some crazy story Mac fed you."

"Not this time. I saw the evidence myself. An exhibit in a science museum. Maybe I oversimplified the explanation a bit, but I told it the best way I could."

"Quite a coincidence that that handy little Viking rock happens to be called sunstone," Nick commented, slinging the duffel bag up onto his back and picking up the ax.

"It's no coincidence," Tracy said as she took the rolled sleeping bag and fitted the rope slings over her shoulders. "Mac heard about sunstone years ago on a prospecting trip to Greenland. He liked the name and decided to use it for the lake and the company." It was all she could do not to add, "So there!"

"The first time I'm in the company library I think I'll look it up," Nick said.

"So much for just believing," Tracy muttered. They were back on the trail, and she was feeling better, she realized. The banter had done it, and Nick had gotten her going so easily, so smoothly. He really was a lovely man—but he was going to pay for his constant doubts, if only in a small way. "Looking it up will confuse you anyway. I tried it."

"Backtracking already?" Nick taunted.

"Not at all. It's just that after a lot of searching I discovered that the sunstone we're talking about isn't the sunstone in the encyclopedia. The one we mean is just a nickname and it should really be spelled as two words. The proper name is . . . is . . ." She cursed under her breath.

"Is?" Nick prompted from behind her.

She turned and glared at him. "I forget. I just forget. Now you really think I'm making this up, but I'm not. You've got me all mixed up with your skepticism."

Grinning, Nick reached out to cup his hand behind her head and plant a kiss on her forehead. "Honey, I believe every word you've ever said to me. Is that better?"

"You don't mean it," Tracy said, grumbling.

"*Now* who's the skeptic?"

She rolled her eyes. "I'm beginning to see why Mac always wants you around when he's involved in important negotiations."

"I'll take that as a compliment, Miss Carlisle."

"It's meant as a compliment, Mr. Corcoran. Now let's get a move on, shall we?" She started along the trail again.

Nick followed her but brought up what seemed to him a valid question. "There's still no break in the clouds. We don't have a Viking with a sunstone, and we can't see the sun, so how do we know which way is south once we've gone around the lake?"

Tracy smiled to herself. "There are lots of techniques. Spiders tend to seek out the south side of trees, for instance."

"Check," Nick said, pretending more disbelief just to keep Tracy riled up. It seemed to be good for her. "I'm to tear along behind you watching for sunbathing spiders. Do they wear garish shirts, drink rum punch, and yell at their tour guides?"

Tracy's lips began to quirk in amusement. "Probably. Be on the alert for the ones wearing little sunglasses."

"I'll do that, sweetheart. What other techniques do you have up your sleeve?"

"Claim posts," Tracy said quite truthfully. "Prospectors' claim posts. There are four to a claim, and they're numbered. The first one is always on the northeast corner of the claim, and each post's tag faces the next post. They're perfect for telling directions if you happen to spot one. So be sure to tell me if you do."

"Got it," Nick said. "Claim posts. Of course, I've never seen one, and I have no idea what to watch for, but who am I to nitpick?"

"Then again," Tracy said as she stopped in her tracks, turned, and pulled a state-of-the-art compass from her pocket, dangling it in front of him, "we could always use this."

Nick's eyes narrowed. "Is that what I think it is, Tracy?"

She batted her eyelashes at him. "Would I have an emergency kit without a compass in it?" she asked sweetly.

He smiled. "I believe I'm going to throttle you. You've had that compass all along?"

"Not in the plane. It was in my bag then."

Nick spoke with exaggerated patience, as if to a small child. "And why weren't we using it before now?"

Tracy mimicked his tone. "Because I didn't need it. Why else?"

"Perhaps to have a little fun with a tenderfoot?"

Her eyes widened in feigned innocence. "Would I do that? I'm the mark who fell for the old clinkers about nails and shoreline and elbow grease, remember?" Suddenly she couldn't keep teasing him. Aware he'd just been trying to keep her mind occupied, she smiled. "Besides, Nick, you're no tenderfoot. You'd never be a tenderfoot anywhere."

He swallowed hard. Staring at her, he decided something: Tracy could state her no-strings terms all she wished, but he wasn't going to cooperate. Complications be damned. She belonged to him and that was that.

Suddenly he realized what the emotion was that had become part of him over the past eighteen hours. It was sheer male territorialism. Tracy was his. Nothing would take her away from him. Not ambition—his or hers—not Walt Cooper, not anything. "I'm a tenderfoot at *this*," he admitted, thinking out loud. He'd been independent, career-driven, emotionally frozen for so long, he was stunned by what was happening to him. He couldn't speak. Didn't dare. Everything was too new, too shocking, too suspect to be put into words.

Tracy searched Nick's hazel eyes and found a startling turmoil within them. What was he thinking? Feeling? Was it possible . . . She didn't dare let herself hope. "Cordierite," she said, the word just popping out.

Nick blinked. "What?"

Tracy smiled feebly. "Cordierite. That's the proper name for the stone the Vikings used. I—I just remembered."

Nick stared at her for another moment, then shook his head as if to clear the cobwebs. "You know those birds that entertained us last night with their giggling songs?"

"You mean the loons?"

"Right," Nick said. "The loons."

"What about them?" Tracy asked.

"Are they relatives of yours?"

Tracy stuck her tongue out at him. "I'll get you for that, Corcoran."

"I'm sure you will, sweetheart." He stepped aside to let her pass and was about to give her a playful smack on the bottom, when she caught him by surprise and got him first.

"An unmitigated brat," he mumbled, falling in step behind her and vowing never to underestimate her again.

They kept up a spirited banter as they steadily headed southward, neither of them willing to lapse into a troubled silence or brood about the problems they had yet to face.

Tracy regaled Nick with anecdotes about Mac, showing him a side to the man he'd never seen, a side he very much wanted to see.

Nick drew her out about herself, her life. She confessed to him that she still carried emotional scars from the time she was eight years old and her father had deserted the family. He told her more than he'd ever told anyone about his own background—about the father he'd never known because, like Tracy's long-absent parent, Eddie Corcoran had taken off without a backward glance for the woman and kids he'd left behind.

Nick revealed to Tracy the secret doubt he'd carried for years, sure he must have done something so terrible his father hadn't wanted him.

And Tracy smiled, at last admitting she still had to fight that particular conviction about herself.

They already were lovers; during their hike they became friends.

The skies cleared and the sun beat down so mercilessly, Nick was grateful for the forest's shade.

There was no sign of Walt Cooper's plane.

"Where is he?" Tracy whispered when she and Nick took a break at yet another sheltered stream.

Nick shook his head. He had no idea what Cooper might be up to, and by now they were too far south to know whether the pilot and his partner had taken off from their lake or were hiding out there. "How about showing me that business with the watch and the sun?" he suggested. It was time for another distraction.

Tracy smiled fondly, well aware what Nick was doing. "Sure," she answered. "It's easy. First you adjust to standard time, so that means you drop an hour from what the watch shows during daylight savings. Then you aim the small hand at the sun—"

"Tracy," Nick interrupted. "I'm not accusing you of another put-on. Honestly I'm not. But you *are* wearing a digital watch. It doesn't have a small hand. It doesn't have any hand. Neither does mine."

Tracy cocked her head to one side and thought about it. "That's true, but you only have to know the time. You can imagine the watch face and the hands in the right position, can't you?"

Nick laughed. "Should've thought of that. Now I feel stupid."

"Don't feel stupid," Tracy said. She waited a beat, then added, "Feel guilty. For doubting me again."

"Now, I *said* I wasn't accusing you . . ."

"But you didn't *mean* it. Anyway, the rest of the lesson. It's two o'clock standard time, so if this were a regular watch face, the two would be here, right?" She raised her arm and pointed to the correct spot on her wrist.

"Right." Nick took hold of the wrist, wondering at its daintiness. After all they'd been through, he still thought of Tracy as fragile. Bending his head, he touched his lips to the inside of her elbow. "Now what?"

It took Tracy a moment to refocus her thoughts. Nick's slightest kiss had a way of addling her brain. "Well . . . um . . . now you point the two toward the sun and follow the shorter arc on the imaginary watch face between the small hand and the twelve. The spot halfway along that arc—in this case the one—points south."

Nick waited for the rest, but Tracy said nothing more. "That's it?" he asked.

"That's it."

"Hey, that's great," he said at last. "You know, I

have read about that trick somewhere, but it sounded more complicated."

Tracy smiled. "Like most things, it really doesn't need to be complicated." She sighed. "And now you and I had better point ourselves due south," Tracy said regretfully. She was getting tired and knew Nick was too. "We have some climbing ahead of us that'll slow us down."

Nick winced as they prepared to take off again. "I thought we had a fair bit of climbing *behind* us."

"We have to reach the height of land before we're even close to the tracks. That much I remember very well. We're not talking about the Continental Divide in the Rockies, but it's a bit of an uphill trek."

"Okay," Nick said with forced cheer. "Let's do it."

Tracy grinned, knowing she'd be grateful for a companion like Nick even if she weren't in love with him.

As she took her place ahead of him on the trail, she realized what she'd silently admitted. She was in love with Nick Corcoran. It wasn't a crush, an infatuation. She loved him. She always would love him, whatever happened once this situation was behind them.

Eight

Tracy mopped her damp forehead with the back of her hand.

"Kind of hot," she commented as she looked around, studying the terrain ahead.

"Kind of," Nick agreed, wiping away rivulets of perspiration from his face with his bared forearm, his jacket long since tucked away in the backpack along with Tracy's sweatshirt. Fortunately the flies weren't bad, but the late afternoon heat was stifling and the long uphill hike hadn't helped.

"I think the worst part is behind us now," Tracy said as she dropped the sleeping bag beside the stream where they'd chosen to stop for their break. "I've been watching the waters for a while; unless I'm wrong, they've begun flowing toward the Great Lakes instead of Hudson Bay. I'd say we've passed the height of land." With an effort at a smile, she added, "From now on it should be all downhill."

"How far to the railroad? Any estimates?"

She shook her head. "I have no idea. Could be a mile, could be ten or even more. The distance between the tracks and the height of land varies."

Nick put down the ax and crouched to splash water over himself, then dug out the single cup he and Tracy shared, dipped it into the stream, and handed it to her. "Are you really this tough?" he asked her. "Or is it an act?"

Tracy drank deeply of the cool, crisp liquid, refilled the cup, and gave it to Nick. "It's an act," she admitted. "For the past hour I've been hallucinating about bubble baths." Frowning as she saw that Nick was rubbing his neck and shoulders, she moved toward him. "Hurts, huh?"

He nodded. "You too?"

"A little."

They took turns massaging away some of the stiffness in each other's muscles, too tired to say much. But by now the silences between them were companionable instead of awkward.

After a too-brief respite they hit the trail again.

"Looks as if you were right," Nick remarked after fifteen minutes. "It's mostly downhill and a lot easier going."

Another fifteen minutes passed. They were approaching a lake. "We'll have to skirt it," Tracy said, betraying none of the emotion she felt. There had been so many obstacles along the way. How could they hope to make it to the tracks in time?

Nick saw her tension but said nothing. They were past trying to distract each other from such disappointments. They just gritted their teeth and forged ahead.

Emerging from the forest, they were glad to find

themselves at one end of the lake instead of the middle, so the detour was short.

After walking for less than ten minutes south of the lake, they heard the rhythmic clacking of steel on steel. It sounded as if it couldn't be far away.

"No!" Tracy cried, breaking into a run. She tore through the forest, ducking heavy branches, getting slapped by lighter ones, almost tripping several times as she clambered over hurdles. "No, no, no!" she said with a sob.

The sleeping bag caught on something. Tracy wriggled out of the ropes and kept going, desperate to reach the tracks before the train went by.

Nick had dropped his burdens by this time too. They wouldn't need them if he and Tracy caught the train.

They didn't catch it.

Tracy stood at the edge of the forest, tears streaming down her cheeks as she watched the last car disappear to the east.

Nick didn't know what to say. He had no words of comfort. Wrapping his arms around Tracy, he simply held her.

"I knew," she said after several moments, her voice muffled against his chest. "I knew we were going to be too late. But I couldn't move any faster. I kept hoping we'd be lucky and the train would be late. Why wasn't it? Why couldn't it have been late? Was that asking so much?"

Nick's mind already had swung into full gear. "What if this *is* a lucky break?" he suggested quietly. "What if Walt finally figured out that as Mac's granddaughter, you just might know your way around this area? Where would he expect you to head?"

Tracy was too upset at first to think, but gradually Nick's words began to make sense. "The tracks," she replied, looking up at him, her eyes red and swollen, her cheeks still wet with tears. "And then, I suppose, he'd expect us to get off at the first town to the east so we could go to the police."

Nick wiped away her tears with the sides of his thumbs. "Then consider this possibility: Cooper could be there waiting for us, or maybe have someone else there." With his lips twitching in a teasing grin, Nick added, "Who knows how many cousins Walt has besides Red?"

Tracy smiled.

Encouraged, Nick developed his theory further. "Cooper probably wouldn't try to recapture us. That's not what I'm suggesting. But he could slap us with a ransom demand for Mac. A simple reversal of plans, that's all. If that happened, Tracy, the man would have us right where he wanted us. We wouldn't dare cross him. And then Mac *would* be in trouble."

"You could be right," Tracy agreed, surprised she hadn't thought of that possibility. "Maybe Mac is safer if Walt is in the dark about where we are."

"I don't think even Cooper is fool enough to compound his problems by hurting Mac," Nick said to reassure her. "Not with a pair of witnesses running around loose. Make sense?"

Tracy nodded, then gave him a dubious look. "You're very convincing. Do you really believe this, or are you just trying to keep me from falling apart?"

"Both," he admitted. "I'll be honest, honey. I didn't believe it enough to suggest we should change our plan, but since fate intervened and changed it for us, I'm almost relieved. And since we can't do much about the situation, we might as well switch to plan B."

"What's plan B?"

Nick grinned. "There's no plan B? Well, shucks, Butch, I thought you were supposed to do the thinkin' while I did the shootin'."

Flinging her arms around his waist, Tracy laughed and hugged him with all her might. "Okay, Sundance. Plan B. Starting with the assumption that Mac isn't in immediate danger, maybe the best thing we can do is go back to that lake we just passed, make camp, have a restful night, and try to meet the morning train heading westbound." She frowned. "Or would we be falling into the same trap?"

Nick remembered something Tracy had said earlier. "You and Mac used to portage from Sunstone Lake to put mail on the trains?"

Tracy closed her eyes and took a deep breath. "You know, I think you'd better do the shootin' *and* the thinkin'. What a dope I am! We don't take the train to any town. We get off south of Sunstone. Sure, we have to hike around the lake, but at least we'd be within striking distance of the lodge. And I really don't think that particular development would occur to Walt." Looking up at Nick again, Tracy's eyes shone with relief and hope and love. "Thanks," she said softly, her voice trembling with emotion. "You sure do know how to perk up my spirits."

"You do pretty perky things to mine too," Nick said. He thought his words were a paltry way to express how Tracy made him feel when she gazed at him lovingly, but the catch in his throat didn't permit more eloquence.

They retraced their trail, picked up the sleeping

bag, backpack, and ax, and strolled to the lake. "Beautiful spot," Nick said as they chose a campsite just a few yards from shore yet sheltered by the forest. "In fact, it's all beautiful. I wish we were here under different conditions. I think I'd really enjoy it."

Bone-weary, they worked slowly at their camp-making chores. Nick chopped wood and then prepared another balsam bed, while Tracy peeled birch bark and gathered twigs for a fire.

"We have an international buffet tonight if you recall," Tracy said playfully as she built her fire on a large, tablelike rock. Though she still was depressed about missing the train, not yet fully convinced Nick's theory was right, she was determined to keep up her spirits. "Reconstituted beef Stroganoff along with the chicken chow mein."

"I recall," Nick said, making a face. "Admittedly, though, it sounds more appetizing now than it did this morning."

"There's nothing like being famished to cause one to acquire more tolerant taste buds," Tracy commented. "And who knows? Perhaps this instant stuff won't be bad at all."

"If it is, I'll pretend I'm eating airline food," Nick said with a smile. "How's the fire doing?"

"Started," Tracy answered. "I'll let it burn for a while. How's the bed coming along?"

Nick laughed as he tossed the sleeping bag over the balsam boughs he'd laid down. "Looks good to me, but I'm no judge. Right about now that flat rock you're sitting on looks inviting."

"Sorry. You can't sleep here," Tracy told him. "This is the kitchen. You're in the bedroom."

"And down there," he said with a dramatic sweep of his hand, "is our en suite spa. The biggest bathtub you ever did see. Had any hallucinations lately, Miss Carlisle?"

Tracy grinned. "I guess I could live without the bubbles, given such a magnificent tub."

Nick walked over to her and pulled her to her feet. "I'd say it's roomy enough for two, wouldn't you?"

"Definitely. But only for two—except perhaps the occasional duck or loon we might tolerate."

"We *have* to tolerate the loons," he said, teasing. "Cousins, you know."

Laughing once again, Tracy eagerly followed him to a large rock that jutted out into the lake, and surprised herself by stripping off her clothes as comfortably as if they were two kids who'd unexpectedly found a swimming hole.

Nick wasn't quite as comfortable. He tried to act nonchalant, but he couldn't help letting his glance linger on Tracy's lovely curves. "You're so pretty," he said. "Every inch of you is just so pretty."

Tracy smiled, another of her long-cherished fantasies coming true as she gazed unashamedly at Nick, memorizing every line of his face and body.

Her rapt expression created such powerful stirrings within Nick, he kept reminding himself he could afford to be patient. There was no need to hurry. They had a whole night—and an entire lake—to themselves.

He went into the water feetfirst and plunged straight down to check the depth. Discovering it was well over his head, he resurfaced to tell Tracy she could jump or dive in safely, only to find that she'd already slid smoothly into a leisurely crawl. "It's wonderful," she said. "Cool but not cold."

Nick swam a short distance along the shoreline until he found a cove where the water was waist-deep, then waded to the narrow beach.

"That's it?" Tracy called. "You've had enough?"

"I forgot something." He went to the duffel bag and moments later was back in the water with a bar of soap and a packet of shampoo.

Tracy treaded water, watching him.

He chose a spot near a conveniently ledged rock, put down the shampoo, and started lathering himself with the soap.

Tracy edged toward him, thinking how much she would enjoy doing that for him, feeling the rippling of muscles under her palms, the silkiness of his soapy chest hair, the warmth and hardness of him.

"Come on over," he said with a casual air he didn't feel. "We'll scrub each other's backs."

Tempted, Tracy nevertheless hesitated.

"What's wrong?" Nick asked after a quick dunking to rinse himself.

"Well . . ." She laughed, embarrassed. "It's just that the water isn't very deep there, and I'm kind of squeamish about touching bottom. I have this irrational, morbid fear of creepy crawlies. It's dumb because it's not as if anything around here is poisonous, and I know water creatures are as skittish as the ones on land, but . . ." Tracy rolled over on her back and floated. She couldn't quite conquer her phobia, yet Nick's body was so inviting, she couldn't look at him anymore.

Nick watched her for a while, luxuriating in the view her pale, voluptuous body presented. Finally watching wasn't enough. He had to touch Tracy. Wading out until the water reached his chest, he called to her again. "Swim over here to me. I'll hold you so you won't have to touch bottom at all."

Pleased that Nick didn't make fun of her silly fears, Tracy thought his solution sounded fine. She turned and did a fast crawl to reach him, letting him take her hands and pull her to him.

"Try floating on your back again," he suggested. The position seemed practical, and he fully appreciated its potential for pleasure. Planting his feet solidly astride on the lake's sandy bottom and sliding one arm under Tracy's body, he palmed the tiny bar of soap and smoothed his hand over her creamy skin in long, sensual strokes. "How's that?" he asked when she smiled up at him in obvious contentment.

"Very nice," she answered, a mischievously sexy expression in her eyes.

Sudden heat coursed through him. "My sentiments exactly," he said in a hoarse voice.

Totally relaxed, Tracy closed her eyes, supported by the water and Nick's cradling arm, soothed and excited by the bold intimacy of his hand.

"Now, a shampoo, milady?" he asked at last. "Sit up and wrap your legs around my waist, sweetheart."

Tracy complied, her body pliant as Nick arranged her in a comfortable but tantalizing position. As she clasped her hands behind his neck, he reached for the packet of shampoo, opened it, and squeezed half the contents onto her hair and half onto his own. "You just hang on," he told her. "I'll do the honors." He lathered Tracy's hair for a while, then his, then hers again, stealing more than a few kisses as he worked. "Now for a rinse," he said. "Ready to go under?"

Tracy squeezed her eyes shut and nodded. It took several dunkings and a great deal of laughter to get rid of all the shampoo, and as Nick smoothed her wet hair back and wiped her eyes, his kisses deepened. Their slick bodies moved and strained with mounting passion until Nick cupped Tracy's buttocks and shifted her position. With a meaningful exchange of looks between them, he plunged into her.

Tracy gasped, overwhelmed by the sweet sensation of fullness, the searing heat, the strange and unexpected thrill of total dependence on Nick's strength. She tipped back her head, arching her spine and gripping his body with her legs while his hands held her in place for his deep, hard thrusts. Her eager surrender created a yielding softness inside her that engulfed him until she was taking everything he could give. "Nick," she cried out as the pleasure became almost unbearable, "This is so . . . it's so wonderful. *You're* so wonderful."

"No, Tracy. You." He was building quickly to climax. "You're wonderful, love. You're everything a man could want. You're—" His arms tightened around her and he was incapable of uttering another word.

Clinging to him, Tracy felt their two bodies contract, and seconds later they were rocketing through heady regions even beyond the galaxies they'd discovered the night before.

Nick's mouth found hers, his tongue delving into its moist recesses as their moans of ecstasy mingled and their bodies throbbed to a single rhythm.

Once again tears streamed down Tracy's cheeks,

but this time they were tears of joy. Nick kissed them away, holding her until their deep pulsations had subsided.

Tracy smiled, nuzzling her face into Nick's damp, fragrant neck. "What was that you were saying yesterday?" she asked dreamily. "About how you're not in the great shape you thought you were?" She laughed with profound contentment. "After the torture we put our bodies through today, you managed—well, what you just managed—and are still managing . . ."

"You inspire Herculean efforts," he answered, a little amazed himself that he'd found such reservoirs of strength. Grinning, he added, "But I have to admit my knees are starting to feel a bit shaky." When Tracy raised her head to smile at him, he gave her a quick kiss. "Lie on your back again, sweetheart."

Too blissful to summon a will of her own, Tracy did as he asked without question, then realized that he was carrying her ashore. "I could swim back to the rock instead," she protested mildly. "There has to be a limit to your expenditure of strength."

"You sound like an accountant," he said with a laugh. "Expenditure of strength?"

An accountant, Tracy mused. Not a bad idea. She'd start by making an inventory of all Nick's assets. The job would take a very long time.

With still more reserves of energy to draw on, Nick refused to put Tracy down when they reached shore. He carried her all the way up to the rock and set her down beside their clothes. "I hate to see you get dressed," he remarked as she pulled on her T-shirt. "Nakedness becomes you."

"And you," she said softly, but tried to shake off

further temptation. "Unfortunately there are still enough mosquitoes buzzing around to make life difficult."

Though Nick regretfully agreed, he decided to try leaving off his perspiration-soaked shirt for a while so he could rinse it and let it dry on the rock.

"Let me put some repellent on you," Tracy offered as he finished wringing out the shirt. She scampered away to get the spray can from the duffel bag and, whirling to run back to Nick, found him right in front of her. "Turn around and close your eyes," she ordered with a surprised laugh.

"Modesty at this point?" Nick asked, eyeing her bare legs.

"Just do what you're told. I'll spray this stuff directly onto your back first." When she'd finished that, she sprayed more of the repellent into her hand. "Now your chest," she murmured with a gleam of anticipation in her eyes.

Nick turned to face her, watching her expression as she smoothed the lotion over him. "How can I be turned on so soon after making love to you, woman? What are you doing to me?"

She put lotion into both her hands and set down the spray can, then flattened her palms over his chest, massaging in the liquid with slow, deep caresses. "I'm enjoying you," she answered at last, lightly circling her fingertips around the dusky brown aureoles of his nipples, then plucking each hardening tip until it stood at attention. "Actually I hired Walt Cooper," she whispered with mock confidentiality. "I was ready to do anything to get you alone so I could have you in my power at last."

Nick was experiencing trouble breathing. "It . . . it

worked," he said raggedly, his hands sliding under her shirt.

Half an hour later, sated for a little while, they made themselves get dressed and cook dinner. "Chicken chow mein?" Nick remarked dubiously as he finished devouring the last bit of food on his plate. "And beef Stroganoff? Could've fooled me. But it was great. Never tasted anything better."

Tracy gathered the dishes to wash them in the stream.

Nick moved to help, impulsively bringing up a subject that was bothering him. "You know, I'm actually grateful to Walt Cooper. Perhaps I'd have opened my eyes eventually, but this caper of his helped."

"You mean you don't believe I hired him?" Tracy asked, teasing.

Nick ignored the question. He had more serious matters on his mind as he crouched beside her, rinsing the dishes she was scrubbing and handing to him. "There was a reason why I didn't want to get involved with you," he told her. "A stupid but effective reason why I didn't want to be attracted to you or even admire you—though I couldn't help it."

"There's something you should know," Tracy put in hastily before he could launch into a heavy and unnecessary discussion. "I'm not your rival, Nick. I never have been."

"Of course you are," he said gently. "There's nothing wrong with that. It's an awkward situation, sure, but we can handle it. Besides, maybe *I'm* not *your* rival. I've been shaken up a bit since yesterday. My priorities are changing as fast as Cecil Berton changes his mind in a heavy board meeting."

Tracy chuckled at Nick's irreverence. "Cecil does tend to sit on the fence until he sees which side Mac takes, doesn't he?

"But *I'm* not on the fence, Nick. Whatever is happening to your priorities, mine aren't changing at all. I'm not interested in succeeding my grandfather to the chairmanship of Sunstone. Never have been."

Nick was determined to be patient. "Honey, I realize you don't want to think about Mac stepping down. I understand. I feel the same way, if you want the truth, and I've felt that way all along. Not just for Mac's sake, or yours, or even the company's—but for mine as well. I could use a lot more seasoning before I try to fill that man's shoes—if anyone could ever hope to do it—so the longer he stays in charge, the better I like it. But we have to face the prospect that someone will succeed him eventually, and the sooner we deal honestly with the fact that you and I are both candidates for the job, the sooner we'll—"

"Nick, listen to me," Tracy said, slapping a fork into his palm like an officious surgical nurse. "I am not, have never been, and hope I never will be a candidate for Mac's job. Don't you realize he hired you for the specific purpose of grooming you to take over someday? Haven't you caught on that you're Mac's troubleshooter not just because he trusts you but because he's making sure you have an intimate knowledge of every division and level of the company? Hasn't it occurred to you that you're based in New York instead of working with him in Chicago so you'll be more inclined to act independently than you would if he were close at hand?" She jumped to her feet and shook her hands vigorously to dry them. "Now I've gone and said too much," she mumbled. "If Mac hasn't explained things to you, I shouldn't have done it."

Nick frowned, taken aback by her rapid-fire remarks. He'd often felt he was being groomed, but the fact that he'd been banished to the East Coast when the main office was in Chicago had made him wonder. "So where does that leave you?" he asked, still hunkered down by the stream, not sure what to think about anything now.

"It has nothing to do with me."

Nick stood up and rested his hands on his hips. "It has everything to do with you. You're Mac's heir."

"So are my mother and sister," Tracy stated, shoving her hands into her back pockets. "Does that mean the three of us should form a triumvirate to take over running Sunstone?"

"That's ridiculous, Tracy. Your mother and sister aren't involved in Sunstone. You are."

"No, I'm not. I'm involved in Carlisle Videos. I'm very lucky that I had a wealthy, powerful grandfather to finance me when I came up with a business plan he considered worth backing. I like what I do, the people I deal with, the excitement of being part of a relatively new industry. I'm also happy to be part of Sunstone. But I don't want to . . . to *be* Sunstone."

Nick couldn't accept that. "I never figured you for a woman who'd back down from a battle just because things got, well, because of a few complications."

"What complications?" she shot back, her voice rising. "I don't see any complications. I see a stubborn male who wants something so much, he can't accept the plain fact that everybody else doesn't want the same thing!"

"So why am I hearing about your lack of ambition now for the first time?" Nick demanded, a sharp edge in his tone.

"My what?" Tracy put her hands on her hips and narrowed her eyes as she glared up at him, totally frustrated by his obstinate refusal to accept the simple truth. "My lack of ambition? I'll have you know I'm *very* ambitious, Nick Corcoran. I just don't happen to think that being the chairman of a corporation is the be-all and end-all of existence!"

"And I suppose I do?"

"Don't you?"

"No, I don't." He hesitated. "Well, maybe I do. Did. Dammit, I— But you still haven't answered my question. Why are you telling me all this now? Isn't this some kind of . . . what's it called, some Cinderella complex thing?"

Tracy clapped her hand to her forehead and raked her fingers through her hair. "Cinderella complex? Cinderella complex? Don't you *dare* haul out that kind of pop psychology to use on me! What does it mean anyway? That I supposedly shy away from success because it might make handsome princes shy away from me? Let me tell you, I have no problem with success. No problem at all! I simply reserve the right to define the word for myself, okay?"

"You have a problem," Nick retorted. "You won't admit even to yourself that you're backing off because you don't want to compete with the man you . . . the man you . . ." He swallowed hard and his words trailed away as he realized he was being presumptuous again.

Tracy stared at him, her frustration fading. So Nick knew she loved him, she thought. And he obviously cared for her, or he wouldn't be so worried about the competition he imagined was between them.

It thrilled her to realize that Nick's protests revealed feelings that might go beyond the casual intimacy of this forest interlude, but she knew she had a problem—two problems, at least: Nick's overabundance of pride and his misguided integrity. He wouldn't beat her to Mac's job by default, and there seemed to be no way to persuade him she honestly wasn't in the running except as a last resort. She'd promised Mac that if he couldn't find anyone else he felt he could trust, she'd step in. He'd found someone else: Nick. Whatever happened on a personal level, she was determined that Nick Corcoran eventually would run Sunstone.

But she was beginning to understand that unless she or Mac could get the truth through Nick's hard head, he would undoubtedly start suspecting that every advancement he made in Sunstone was due to his relationship with the boss's granddaughter—unless he decided to solve the problem by choosing not to *have* a relationship with her once they were back in civilization, and reality, along with Tanya the Jungle Girl, returned.

The whole thing was too much for Tracy to worry about at the moment. "You were right in the first place," she said quietly, reaching up to touch her hand to Nick's cheek. "We'll handle this . . . this awkward situation. But not tonight, okay?"

Nick grimaced and pulled her into his arms. He felt like kicking himself. "Tracy, you'll soon learn, if you don't already know, that one of my less admirable qualities is knuckleheaded impatience. I want instant solutions. Chicken-chow-mein answers. But I guess some things aren't that easy." Pressing his lips to Tracy's temple, he took a deep breath and let it out slowly, wishing he'd kept his mouth shut about their corporate problems. She had enough on her mind.

Once the dust had settled, he promised himself, he would make her deal with their rivalry honestly. There was no way he'd allow her to bow out and leave the field to him. He appreciated her generosity of spirit, but that wasn't the way he operated.

He felt an odd tug of wistfulness. A few moments earlier he'd started to tell Tracy she was backing off because she wouldn't compete with the man she loved.

Premature and irrational as it was, he wished she'd supplied the final word, the one he hadn't dared to say.

Nine

A loon's haunting cry woke Nick just after dawn.

Stirring in his arms as the muted giggle echoed across the lake again, Tracy smiled up at him. "Listen," she whispered. "They're playing our song."

Caught in an unguarded moment, Nick laughed softly, enfolded her against him, and forgot to suppress the phrase that begged to be spoken. "I love you, Tracy," he told her.

In her half sleep his words came as no surprise. They were part of the flow of her dreams. "I love you too," she said, a confession that seemed as natural and easy as it was inevitable.

They dozed off again, lulled by the gentle music of the forest.

When Nick awakened, he found that Tracy had turned and rolled away from him enough so that he could move without disturbing her.

As he sat up he recalled his early-morning declaration of love and smiled at the memory of Tracy's response.

So easy, he mused. It had been so easy to say the words he'd always considered forbidden. To tell a woman he loved her just to get her into bed had never been his style. To tell a woman he loved her and mean it? That possibility had seemed increasingly unlikely as a passing parade of female companions had inspired nothing stronger in him than physical desire or, at best, mild affection.

He watched Tracy as she slept, her breathing deep and even, her lips curved in a secret smile, her tousled hair a golden aura framing her delicate features.

I love you, Nick repeated silently.

With great care he got to his feet without waking Tracy. He had to *do* something. Besieged by his usual impatience, he wanted to get on the move again, to rescue Mac, find out who had fed Walt Cooper his information, deal with that situation, and then decide how to handle all the other minor obstacles to perfect happiness. And he wanted to do it all immediately.

Yet he wished he could linger with Tracy in their own special utopia, making love and fashioning their own uncomplicated existence.

A bracing dip in the lake seemed like the best way to clear his head.

He went down to the rock at the deep part of the shoreline, peeled off his clothes, and slid silently into the water.

Refreshing, he told himself as his body discovered how cold a northern lake could become overnight.

Gradually growing accustomed to the temperature, he swam out to a tiny island and back to the shallow cove where he and Tracy had made love.

Smiling at the recollection, he waded ashore, went

up to the rock where he'd left his clothes, and as soon as the cool morning air had dried him, got dressed.

He was fastening his belt buckle when he noticed the canoe.

Made of birch bark, it had been dragged to a secluded spot and hidden upside down among the tall grasses and cattails.

Nick was sure the canoe hadn't been there the night before.

Hurrying quietly back toward camp, he scanned the surrounding forest with a sick dread that Walt Cooper or someone he'd hired had tracked them after all. He saw no one, but his every muscle and sinew was taut, braced for trouble.

When he was close enough to see Tracy still sleeping peacefully, Nick hesitated, not sure whether to approach her.

He chose to leave her sleeping for the moment. They had a visitor, but Nick didn't know where he was. Waking Tracy could send up an alert that would bring their uninvited guest running.

Inching over to the backpack, he reached into its outside pocket for Red's gun.

It was gone.

Now there was no choice. He had to wake Tracy. For the second time he cursed his stupidity over that gun. He'd been too relaxed, too sure they hadn't been tracked. He'd let down his guard, and now he and Tracy were vulnerable.

Before he roused Tracy, Nick made a quick scan of the surrounding trees again. What he saw brought his heart to a screeching halt.

A man was moving through the forest toward the

campsite—a very large man, well over six feet tall with muscular arms and wide shoulders. As the man drew closer, Nick saw he had a craggy face, deeply tanned and etched with lines, dominated by dark eyes and framed by a dramatic mass of white, tightly curled hair that stood out like a profusion of electrically charged cotton balls.

Another of Walt Cooper's weird cousins, Nick wondered as he looked around for something to use as a weapon and cursed himself all over again for being so careless with Red's gun.

He spied a thick branch lying almost within reach and moved quietly, stretching out his arm until he could curl his fingers around the makeshift club and draw it toward him. Tension mounted inside him as every step he took threatened to create a sound that would draw the giant's attention.

Finally, branch in hand, he took cover behind the trees and with painful slowness circled around behind the massive form that had by now reached the campsite.

With sickening dread Nick saw Red's gun tucked into the waistband of the man's khaki pants.

That did it. The man meant trouble. Put him out of action first, Nick told himself. Ask questions later.

Clutching his gnarled mace in two hands, he raised it and lunged, slamming it down on the intruder's huge shoulder.

The man turned slowly, not even swaying under the force of the blow. Nick tried another strike, but a large arm came up and easily knocked the weapon aside.

Nick watched in horror as the branch crumbled.

its useless fragments scattering on the ground as Nick stared at it, then at his opponent.

Understanding dawned slowly. The branch was dry-rotted. His stomach lurched as he realized he'd lost the element of surprise. He didn't have much else going for him.

Tracy, hearing the commotion, sat up with a start. When she saw what was happening she leapt to her feet. "Nick!"

"Run, Tracy!" he shouted without looking back at her. "Get out of here!" He took a flying leap, determined to give Tracy a chance to escape. But landing on the great, roughhewn form was like crashing into a pile of bricks. "Tracy, move it!" he yelled raggedly as soon as he'd caught his breath.

"Nick, no!" Tracy cried, dashing over to the two men and trying to drag Nick off the giant's body.

"What the hell's the matter with you!" he hollered at her. "Get out of here, I said!" Maybe, just maybe he could hold the man back long enough to give Tracy time to escape. Then again, he thought as he was suddenly shaken, bounced, and whirled like a rodeo clown on a crazed bull, maybe not.

And Tracy wasn't helping by clawing at his legs and screaming senselessly at him.

Finally her words filtered through. "Nick, listen to me! It's all right! Let go, Nick. He won't hurt us!"

Nick could only grunt. By this time he was holding on for dear life.

Tracy realized she was talking to the wrong man. She ran around the pair to look up into the familiar, dear face. "Lord Jon, please put Nick down. He was only trying to protect me."

The bouncing stopped at last, and Nick jumped clear.

"Trying to protect you from me?" the man Tracy had called Lord Jon questioned with a deep, cultured British accent.

"That's why he was shouting at me to run," Tracy explained.

Lord Jon's dark eyes gave Nick a quick perusal. "When I arrived early this morning, I did assume you two were . . . well, shall we say, friends. And I had decided that this young man must be the Corcoran lad who was kidnapped with you, Tracy, which is why I tried not to cause any harm. However, when one is attacked, even with a disintegrating weapon, self-defense becomes quite necessary." He smiled at Nick. "I do admire you, young man. Such spunk. I don't believe anyone has tried pitting himself against me since I gave young Jack Dempsey his first pugilistic lesson."

Nick was utterly baffled. "How do you know about the kidnapping? What were you doing skulking around in the woods? What happened to the gun?"

"I shall explain in good time how I know about the kidnapping," Lord Jon said pleasantly. "And I was not skulking. I was examining some badly stricken maple trees. The species is in real peril, you know. Dreadful waste. Oh, and your gun? Why, I removed it, of course. You were both sleeping soundly when I arrived, and as I was here to watch over you, I hardly imagined you would need firearms. And experience has taught me that my appearance for some reason gives rise to fear. Panic, in fact. More than once I've been obliged to sidestep bullets aimed at me under such circumstances." Turning to Tracy,

Lord Jon beamed with obvious affection and opened his arms to her.

She went to him, burying her face in his broad chest. "You've seen Mac, haven't you. Is he all right?"

"He was in tip-top shape as of yesterday morning," Lord Jon answered, patting her back. "Concerned about you, of course, but confident that you had managed to elude those hoodlums."

Nick wondered if he still was asleep and having a slightly eccentric dream. "Would you folks like to fill me in? What's going on here?" he asked quietly.

Lord Jon released Tracy, but she held his hand. "This is one of Mac's oldest and dearest friends," she told Nick. "Lord Jon Carruthers. Our answer to Paul Bunyan."

"Hardly," Lord Jon said with a modest smile as he thrust out his hand to Nick. "At least, not since I retired from the lumber camps some thirty years ago. And you are, it seems, Nicholas Corcoran, William's young protégé."

Nick and Tracy exchanged a glance as Nick's attention was caught by the word *protégé*. Perhaps Tracy was right, he thought. Maybe Mac really was grooming him.

Suddenly he balked at the idea. It wasn't fair to Tracy. She was capable, competent, loyal. Why should she be cheated? Even if she were willing to cheat herself by pretending she'd never wanted to succeed her grandfather.

"How did you find us?" Tracy asked, bringing Nick's thoughts back to the present.

Nick wanted his original question answered. "How did you know what happened?"

"First," Lord Jon said, "I've brought some food.

You are hungry, are you not? I have some of Eleanor's scones with her famous wild strawberry jam."

"Eleanor?" Nick repeated, beginning again to doubt the reality of all this. "Scones? Strawberry jam?"

"You know women," Lord Jon said to him. "When my wife learned I was coming to find you, she insisted on sending a treat. Not that I minded. A few scones, especially Eleanor's, are no great burden in my pack, which I've left behind a rock near your campfire. Shall we?"

Nick followed mutely as they trooped back to the campsite.

Lord Jon built a fire while Tracy freshened up by the stream and Nick rolled up the sleeping bag. "I also brought tea," Lord Jon said. "With all there is to be done today, we must begin with tea."

Tracy filled one of the pots with water and put it on the fire to boil. "Now tell us, Lord Jon. Did Mac send up a flare or something?"

"Several flares," Lord Jon answered. "That was the night before last. The signal was an old one, but I still remembered it from . . . when? Can it really be fifteen years since your grandfather and I worked out those signals for the flares? At any rate, he sent up three, then waited exactly ten minutes before sending the fourth. Half an hour later he repeated the signal, which meant he wanted to see me but there was no immediate emergency, so I need not travel through the forest in the dark. I went to him first thing the next morning. Yesterday."

"You'd worked all that out fifteen years ago?" Nick asked as he sat down opposite their visitor. "Why? And how did you remember?"

Lord Jon gave him a tolerant smile. "William and I

have been through many an adventure together, young man, and living as Eleanor and I do just a few miles to the east of Sunstone Lake, a set of signals between neighbors seemed a sensible precaution. I remembered them simply because I happen to have quite a good memory."

"Lord Jon really *is* a lord," Tracy put in, seeing how perplexed Nick was by her grandfather's old friend. "Oxford-educated too," she added. "He turned over his estate in England to his younger brother forty years ago, but everyone still refers to him by his title." She smiled nervously at Lord Jon. "If Nick seems a little hesitant, it's because he isn't sure what to believe anymore."

"You have doubts about something, young man?" Lord Jon asked, one brow raised in amusement.

"Why should I have doubts?" Nick answered with a grin. "An Oxford-educated British aristocrat comes by birch bark canoe to rescue us in a remote area of wilderness after being summoned by flare signals worked out fifteen years ago? Doubts? About what?" More seriously he added, "But I *would* like to know how you managed to locate us. The proverbial needle in a haystack seems like an easier proposition."

"Logic, son. Logic."

"Why do I feel like I'm Dr. Watson and you're Sherlock Holmes?" Nick remarked, beginning to see a glimmer of humor in the whole situation.

Lord Jon smiled. "Ah, yes. My good friend Conan Doyle. Dear old Binkie—that's what Mother called him, you know. I've no idea why. Such an amusing fellow though. Loved visiting us in the country, said it brought him closer to the spirits. Rather a superstitious chap, he was."

There was a ring of truth to Lord Jon's remarks; Nick had read about the Sherlock Holmes author's interest in spiritualism. But the timing seemed wrong. "You knew Conan Doyle? I thought he died in the twenties?"

"Nineteen-thirty, to be precise," Lord Jon replied. "And yes, I knew him. I was just a boy, of course."

Nick was staring at Lord Jon in utter amazement, and Tracy exploded into peals of laughter. "Nick, I can't bear it anymore! You thought *I* was bad? This is the man who likes nothing better than to sit around with Mac seeing which one of them can spin the most outrageous yarn!" She turned to Lord Jon and gave him a stern look. "Now, will you explain how you tracked us down?"

Nick looked at the ground, shaking his head and laughing. He'd been royally had.

Lord Jon winked at Tracy. "I sent out my retriever pigeon."

"Not even *this* tenderfoot will buy retriever pigeons," Nick said with feigned exasperation. "Let's try again. What was that you'd started to say a few minutes ago about logic?"

Tracy smiled at Nick. If she weren't already in love with him, his good humor in the face of such relentless leg-pulling would have conquered her heart.

Lord Jon took a cup from his backpack and set it beside the two Tracy had put out. "All right," he said as he poured the tea. "I shall explain seriously. As I said, tracking was"—he winked at Nick—"elementary, my dear boy."

Nick grinned but said nothing. Silence was more prudent, he thought.

Handing out the teacups, then the scones he'd

brought, Lord Jon continued. "When I arrived at the lodge, William told me about his visit from this Cooper chap. He also explained that he believed you youngsters had effected an escape." As he sat down with his tea, Lord Jon inclined his head toward Tracy in a sort of bow. "That story you concocted for your kidnappers was smashing. Worthy of a real woodsman, my girl."

Nick glanced at Tracy. The way she beamed at the compliment made him want to hug her forever.

Sipping his tea, Lord Jon explained everything: How Mac, with a few casual questions and well-placed comments, had managed to extract from Walt Cooper several small but vital details about the deserted cabin hideout; how Mac had sent Walt Cooper back with a camera to take a picture of his captives as proof that he had them, how he'd noted the direction of the aircraft as Walt took off.

"William and I know this country intimately," Lord Jon said. "It was quite simple to deduce the probable location of that cabin, and even easier to guess that you would head straight south toward the railroad tracks. You moved a tad more quickly than I had estimated, or I would have found you much sooner. You were in quite a hurry. Concerned about William, I should imagine."

"Worried sick," Tracy said. "If Walt Cooper can't have us, he'll go after Mac. We . . . I have to get back to the lodge."

"We," Nick corrected her.

Lord Jon nodded. "William and I anticipated that reaction." He glanced at Nick approvingly. "From both of you. Naturally William would prefer that I simply lead you to safety while he takes care of himself, but I knew you would reject such a craven alternative. And rightly so."

"We thought we'd flag down the westbound train and get off south of Sunstone Lake," Tracy said.

"A splendid plan," Lord Jon responded. "Especially if you had no other option. However, by the time one waits for the train, travels on it to the lake, circumvents it . . . We happen to be almost due east of the lodge now. We would make far better time simply going by canoe and portage."

Nick understood the logic but he shifted uncomfortably. He'd seen Lord Jon's canoe. It didn't look as if it would support much weight. Still, he thought, if it meant getting to Mac sooner . . . "These scones are great," he said, making up his mind to go along cheerfully with whatever method of travel Tracy and Lord Jon chose. "And Eleanor's wild strawberry jam would make you a fortune if it were marketed in New York's trendy shops."

"Oh, it is," Lord Jon said, his expression absolutely deadpan as he finished his tea and started dousing the fire with water from the stream.

Tracy rolled her eyes but saw Nick's mouth twitching with humor. He didn't need to be rescued this time, she decided.

"Come on," Nick said, picking up a stick to stir the embers to mud as he'd seen Tracy do to their other campfires. "You aren't going to tell me that the Strawberry Fields Forever line of gourmet food is Eleanor's!"

"Enough!" Tracy said. "Lord Jon, we're creating a monster!" She smiled at Nick. "The honest, straightforward Nick Corcoran is just fine, okay?"

Nick winked at her. "Okay," he said, pretending to

be contrite. He turned to Lord Jon. "Does Mac know what he'll do if Walt tries to take him hostage? Is Mac armed? Has he sent for help?"

"William wouldn't send for help until he was certain you were safe," Lord Jon said. "Nor will he arm or defend himself in any way as long as there is any chance you youngsters are still being held."

"I knew that," Tracy said quietly. "That's why we have to get to him as quickly as possible." She finished her tea and jumped to her feet, looking around the campsite. "We should be able to jettison some of this stuff," she added. "The sleeping bag, for instance. And a lot of what's in the pack."

"Any idea what we'll do if Cooper's already at the lodge when we arrive?" Nick asked Lord Jon. "I'm not too crazy about having Tracy walk into an ambush." He hadn't forgotten Cooper's sleazy remark about having fun with her.

"We can talk things over on the way," Lord Jon said. "But yes, I have a few ideas." Glancing at Tracy's suddenly strained face, he handed Nick the gun he'd taken earlier and winked at him. "After all, I've promised Eleanor we'll all be there for a late lunch today. Including William. And in forty years of wedded bliss, I believe I can say without fear of contradiction that I have never broken a promise to my Eleanor."

Nick checked the gun, making sure the safety was on, and tucked it into his waistband. He smiled at the man he now considered a friend—especially since Lord Jon's confidence had erased some of the tension from Tracy's expression. "You know," he said with complete sincerity, "I can hardly wait to meet your Eleanor."

Lord Jon clapped him on the back. "So you shall, my boy. And now we must go."

One of Lord Jon's ideas became apparent when he and Nick flipped the canoe over. A large bow and a quiver filled with arrows was wedged under the seats.

As they started across the lake in the fragile birch-bark craft—built by Lord Jon himself, Nick learned to his increasing consternation—Nick's heart sank, and he was sure they would all be doing the same thing within seconds.

But the canoe was hardier than it looked, and not as lightweight as it appeared, Nick discovered when he helped carry it on the first portage. He soon got the hang of moving through the forest with a canoe over his head—and felt more than a little proud of the accomplishment. The second portage was easier. As they crossed the third lake, Nick helped with the paddling and glowed when Lord Jon called him a natural.

Nick was amazed to find he liked canoeing, liked the feel of the paddle in his hands, the challenge of dipping it silently into the lake, of pulling it back just so, of lifting it over the surface and hearing the melodic plops of water that dripped off its edges. He even was proud of the slight ache in his back.

Before long he began to understand how men like Mac and Lord Jon could make a person aspire to be a "real woodsman." And he basked in Tracy's delight at his newfound prowess.

Finally they reached a lake that seemed much larger than any of the others. "Sunstone," Tracy told Nick in a clipped, tense voice.

Hugging the shore, they paddled to a spot Lord Jon silently indicated and beached the canoe. "The lodge overlooks the bay just beyond that point of land," Tracy said in a low voice.

Moving through the dense bush slowly, carefully, quietly, they got close enough to see the lodge.

Walt Cooper's Cessna was at the dock.

Tracy, following behind Lord Jon and Nick, bit down on her trembling lower lip, then smiled at Nick when he glanced back at her with a concerned expression on his face.

She nodded and formed a circle with her thumb and index finger in an "everything's-okay" gesture.

Under cover of the forest, they paralleled the shoreline of the bay until they were able to see Mac. He was standing against the railing of the deck, looking out over the lake.

Behind him, sitting in a lounge chair, swigging a bottle of beer, was Red.

Lying across Red's knees and clutched in his free hand was a sawed-off shotgun.

Ten

"That scruffy knave behind William," Lord Jon said in a low voice. "Surely that can't be your Mr. Cooper."

Nick shook his head. "That's Cooper's little helper," he said quietly. "Name's Red." Lord Jon already had been filled in on the details of what had happened in the cabin.

"Red? For his hair, one assumes? How very original," Lord Jon said. "Well, whatever. It should be to our advantage that the dolt is in view and can be easily disarmed. However . . ."

"Where's Walt Cooper?" Nick asked, supplying the rest of Lord Jon's question. "There's no sense tipping our hand until we know."

"We need to smoke Walt out," Tracy whispered. "I can do that. I'll go in pretending I've made my way back to the lodge alone—"

Nick cut her words short. "Forget it, Tracy. If anyone goes in there to get Cooper's attention, it'll be me."

"Red would shoot you on sight," Tracy argued. "You'd be a liability as a hostage. I'd be an asset. I'm the granddaughter, remember? Handy to have around to keep Mac under control and no threat myself. After all, I'm just a girl, remember? Small and fluttering and helpless." She smiled sweetly and batted her eyelashes.

Nick shook his head. "I don't imagine those two characters still think of you in those terms, Tracy. You wouldn't get away with your act a second time."

"Sure I would. They're slow learners. I'm telling you, Nick, someone has to walk right up to that deck to attract Walt's attention, and I'm the only one who can hope to get away with it."

"I won't let you do it," Nick insisted. "Give me all the reasons you like, but I won't let you take one step toward that lodge, understand?"

Tracy looked him straight in the eye. "I'm going, Nick."

"You're not going, Tracy," Nick said through clenched teeth, his tone low but intense. "Do you think you're invincible or something?"

"No, but I can take care of myself in this particular situation."

"Oh, sure. Go up against a sawed-off shotgun and Walt's Magnum completely unarmed and vulnerable. I said forget it, Tracy. Just forget it."

"Tracy," Lord Jon said.

She turned to look at him, and her hand instinctively shot up as Lord Jon calmly tossed something to her.

Nick gasped as her fingers gripped the handle of a very large, very lethal-looking hunting knife.

"She needn't be unarmed, young man," Lord Jon

said with a smile, handing Tracy his leather sheath. "As you can see, Tracy is quite adept with a knife, and her reflexes are excellent. From childhood she has spent many a night at solitary target practice, bored with the endless, boasting reminiscences of men around a campfire. Why, for a time I suspected her secret ambition was to join a circus."

"Thanks, Lord Jon," Tracy said as she clipped the sheath to the back of her jeans, slid the blade into it, and pulled her T-shirt down to cover the weapon. "I don't expect to have any need for this, but it'll be a comfort." She looked at Nick. "You know I'm the right one to do this, don't you?"

He did know it. If he tried to approach the deck, most likely he *would* be shot, which wouldn't help Mac or anyone else. Nick finally nodded, conceding defeat as he saw the familiar set to her jaw. "But I hate it, Tracy. And you have to promise me you won't take any dumb chances like trying to pull that knife on Red or trading smart quips with Cooper, or—"

"I'm going to play wounded bird," Tracy interrupted. "Nothing more." She forced herself to smile confidently. "Don't worry, Sundance, I'm counting on my partners to do the shootin'." Turning quickly, before she could lose her courage, she strode toward the lodge deck, bending to scoop up a bit of dirt to smear on her face and arms and clothes, then thoroughly messing up her hair. If she was going to be a wounded bird, she might as well look the part.

"Mac!" she cried out as she emerged from the woods and stumbled up the deck stairs. "Mac, it's Tracy! Mac, help me!" Running to her grandfather, she pretended to sob against his chest as he wrapped his arms around her and held her so tight, she hardly could breathe.

"Hey, what the . . . where'd she come from!" Red stuttered, scrambling to his feet and waving the shotgun uncertainly.

Looking up as if startled, she stared at the gun. "Mac," she said in a small voice that came naturally from her real fear and from seeing Mac's gray, drawn face. He hadn't looked that way since her grandmother's death. Worried about him, Tracy couldn't say another word for a moment. Then she remembered: She had to keep talking, distracting Red. "Mac, you don't mean . . . they're here?" she cried. "I thought I'd . . . oh, no! Oh, please, no!" She wondered if she was overacting, but Red seemed to be going for it.

"Thought you got away, huh?" Red put in, so pleased with the new development, it was obvious he was taking personal credit for it. Then he scowled. "Where's the guy?"

Tracy sniffled. "I had to leave him in the bush. He fell and broke his leg." Looking up at Mac, she took a deep, shuddering breath. "I thought I'd be safe if I got back to you," she said, her accusing tone designed to let him know this was an act.

"Sorry, honey," Mac said. "I guess I let you down this time."

He sounded utterly defeated, and he seemed to have aged. Tracy leaned back against him so he'd feel the knife at her waist and know they were far from beaten.

If Mac realized she had a knife, he didn't show it. He just stood there looking old.

"Well now," Red crowed, "Walt's sure gonna be happy about this. We got two for one."

Tracy wiped her eyes and glared at Red. "Where *is* your charming cousin anyway?"

"Puttin' some supplies in the plane. We were plannin' to take the old geezer to another hideout, so I guess you can come along too."

She looked at her grandfather. "Don't let them, Mac! Don't let them take us! Can't you fight them?"

"Sure," Red said. "You two oughta be able to put up a real good fight. Gramps'll bite me with his false teeth, an' you'll give me one of them looks to kill." He giggled, enjoying his own brand of wit.

"My grandfather does *not* have false teeth!" Tracy yelled, genuinely irritated. She was deeply upset by Mac's inertia. He seemed to have lost his spirit.

A shrill whistle from the lake made Red give a little start. "That's my signal," he said, excitedly waving the gun at Tracy and Mac and using it to point to the deck's steps. "We gotta go now. Don't try anything neither. I'm not gonna fall for no more tricks, see?"

Tracy went ahead of Mac, her body masked by his so she could reach behind her and put her hand on the hilt of the knife. She didn't want to have to use the thing, but if something had gone wrong, if Nick and Lord Jon had been put out of commission somehow . . .

"Hurry it up," Red prompted. "I can't wait to see Walt's face when he finds out what I got for him. Man, he's just gonna—"

Red's words stopped so abruptly both Mac and Tracy turned to look at him.

His eyes were huge, and he seemed to be trying to see behind him. The muzzle of a gun was on his temple.

"Nicely done," Mac said calmly, smiling at Nick without any show of surprise.

Tracy stared at her grandfather. The years had dropped away, the tension lines were gone, the blue eyes had their normal twinkle. She breathed a deep sigh of relief, realizing Mac was still a master leg-puller. Even she'd been taken in by his act.

Nick grinned tightly. "Hand the old geezer the shotgun, Red," he ordered, his menacing tone heavily laced with sarcasm.

"Thought you had a broken leg," Red muttered, carefully giving Mac the weapon.

"The lady just isn't fair, is she," Nick said, sticking his gun back into the waistband of his jeans now that Mac was covering Red. "Lying to you all the time the way she does. I can't seem to break her of the habit. Tracy, honey, do you think you can find some rope?"

"I can probably handle that," she said with a grin. "In the storeroom at the back of the lodge?" she asked Mac. Noticing her grandfather's bemused smile as he glanced at Nick, she realized how profoundly some things had changed since three mornings ago.

"Aw, are you gonna tie me up again?" Red protested, recapturing Mac's attention. "My cousin'll skin me alive. Walt's still mad at me from the last time."

"Call him," Mac said calmly.

Red stared at him. "What?"

"Call him," Mac repeated. "Get Cooper back here."

"No way, man." Red turned pale. "You know what he'll do to me if I double-cross him like that?"

Mac smiled. "No, but I know what *I'll* do to you if you don't. In fact, I'd be happy for the excuse. In fact, I don't even *need* an excuse." Mac placed the shotgun on the table and advanced slowly toward the smaller man, rolling up his shirt-sleeves to reveal muscular arms that made Red's eyes bulge half out of their sockets. "Let's just see how much damage an old geezer can do, shall we?" Mac said, curling his right hand into a fist and drawing it back for what promised to be a powerful blow.

"Walt!" Red screeched. "I need you up here! Come quick!"

Mac lowered his hand, sadly shaking his head. "A man can't have any fun nowadays."

Seeing his opportunity, Red tried to bolt toward the steps. He ran straight into Mac's fist, which shot out with lightning speed.

"Nicely done," Nick said, echoing Mac's earlier compliment to him. Red crumpled to the deck. "But we'd better get him inside," Nick added.

They each took one of Red's arms and hauled his limp body into the lodge.

"I'll tie him up while you go back out and greet Walt," Tracy said, her smile dazzling. She dashed toward the rear of the house to get the rope from the storage room.

"You two youngsters seem to have become friends," Mac remarked.

Nick grinned. "You might put it that way. Why don't you stay here and let Tracy bring you up-to-date? Lord Jon's out in the bush somewhere; he and I can handle Cooper." Reaching out to the table, Nick took the shotgun and gave it to Mac. "Just keep this handy in the unlikely event something goes wrong, all right?"

Mac nodded. "Be careful, Nick," he said quietly. "And thanks for taking good care of my little girl."

With a laugh Nick shook his head. "Thanks for giving me a little girl who could take such good care of *me*!" Then he went out onto the deck and vaulted over the railing to disappear into the thickets, wondering just where Lord Jon was hiding.

Cooper hadn't come running at Red's call. Nick didn't like that. It meant the man was suspicious.

Half expecting Walt to ambush him, Nick tensed up at every sound as he moved toward the dock, his gun ready. After nearly three days in the forest he still wasn't used to all the sounds. A partridge nearly got its head blown off as he whirled on it. A scolding chipmunk triggered a wild burst of adrenaline that made Nick's blood pound in his head. A low-hanging branch caught his shirt, and he was sure Cooper had grabbed him.

Calm down, he told himself. Just stay cool.

He was almost at the lake when he heard the thudding of footsteps on the dock followed by Walt Cooper's outraged yell. An instant later Nick saw the reason for Cooper's fury. Walt was on the dock a few feet from his plane, trying to get to it, obviously planning to climb in and take off without waiting for Red. But every time he took a step toward the Cessna an arrow whizzed past his head.

"What the hell is this!" Walt hollered, staring aghast at an arrow stuck into the dock right at his feet, the shaft still quivering. "Who's out there? You trying to play cowboys and Indians or something?" He was waving his gun as he took a desperate leap toward the plane. Another arrow hissed by him, and he shot into the trees. "Come on! What are you, some kind of madman? Cut it out!" He kept trying for the plane, shooting erratically every time an arrow stopped him. Finally he decided to retreat, crouching and heading back along the dock toward the bush.

Nick braced himself. Cooper was dashing straight toward him but hadn't spotted him yet.

A sudden rustle of trees behind him made Nick pivot, wondering if he was aiming his gun at another cranky chipmunk.

Tracy hit the ground instantly, realizing almost too late that catching up to Nick hadn't been smart.

Nick felt the blood drain from his face. He swung back toward Walt, willing himself to pull the trigger if necessary.

But one of Lord Jon's arrows had cut off Cooper's retreat. Walt screamed with rage, his face purple and contorted. He started shooting again, pulling the trigger over and over until it occurred to him he was hearing only impotent clicks. He glared at the gun as if it had betrayed him.

"Tracy," Nick muttered. "I ought to—"

"I know, I know," she interrupted. "I was stupid. I was also terrified when I heard those gunshots. I couldn't stay in the lodge wondering if you were hurt. I just couldn't, all right? Red's tied up, by the way. Mac's still watching him."

"You see where those arrows are coming from?" Nick asked abruptly. Yet another had hissed by Walt's shoulder when he'd tried to reload his gun.

Tracy nodded, smiling as she saw that Walt had been rendered absolutely immobile by the steady hail of arrows.

Nick motioned with a quick inclination of his head. "Then get over there with Lord Jon and stay with him. And if you try walking into danger one more time, Tracy Carlisle, you'll have more of it than you can handle. All from me, understand?"

Reacting instantly, Tracy went.

Nick stepped out of the bush, holding his gun straight out in front of him with both hands. Walt saw him and started pulling the trigger of his Magnum again as if hoping to find a bullet in there somewhere.

Nick walked slowly toward him. "Who hired you, Cooper? Who gave you the information you needed?"

Walt panicked, throwing his gun at Nick, missing him but using the momentary distraction to drop down and execute a flying tackle, catching Nick around the knees and bringing him down.

Tracy was watching from her safe vantage point with Lord Jon. When she saw Nick's gun slip from his grasp, she instinctively leapt forward, propelled by fear for him.

But Nick managed to throw the weapon into the bush, and as Walt reached up to try to catch the gun, Nick grasped his flailing arm and neatly flipped the man onto his back. Grabbing a fistful of shirt, he raised Walt up to face him. "Now. Who paid you?"

Too desperate or stubborn or foolish to know when he'd been beaten, Walt summoned all his strength to try to throw Nick off.

It didn't work. "Dammit, Cooper," Nick shouted. "Now you've made me mad!" It took just one punch. Nick frowned at the unconscious man. "I guess we'll just have to ask him later."

Tracy sat cross-legged on the ground watching Nick. He prowled in constant circles around the huge hemlock tree where Red and Walt were secured on opposite sides to the thick trunk.

Tracy still was getting used to a different Nick Corcoran than the gentle, affectionate man she'd come to know over the past days. She was seeing the hard, frightening Nick. The one who got to the bottom of things. Who didn't let anybody get away with anything.

She admired this Nick Corcoran. She thrilled to his sheer physical strength as much because he used it sparingly, without fuss, as because he had it to draw on.

But she was troubled—foolishly, she hoped. She couldn't help fearing that life would return to normal now. What if Nick began remembering all the reasons he had to resent her? What if his steely manner had returned to stay? Wasn't this the Nick who preferred a Tanya to a Tracy?

Even in her moments of anxiety she was fascinated by him, almost seeing the workings of his mind as it sorted bits of information and tried to fit them into some kind of pattern, some sort of answer to his questions.

There were no answers from Red or Walt, no matter how many questions were thrown at them. Walt was stubbornly silent. Red either knew nothing or was too cowed by his cousin to speak up. Neither would say who had hired them. Neither would even explain what the ransom demand would have been had their scheme worked.

"Why the closed mouths?" Nick asked them. "Why would you be willing to face prison while the real criminal gets off scot-free?" When he was greeted by only more silence, he sighed heavily and turned to

Mac. "What are we going to do with these characters? We can't get anything out of them, so we might as well quit trying."

Mac leaned his foot on a nearby log and looked down at the two men. "We'll just have to leave them here and send the authorities to pick them up."

Tracy saw Red's eyes fill with fright at Mac's words. He looked around at the place where he and Walt would be left to wait for the police. Following his gaze, Tracy realized he was seeing the forest she'd always loved, her own private fiefdom several hundred yards behind Sunstone Lodge as hostile, shadowy, filled with terrors.

Nick perched on a rock and folded his arms over his chest, looking steadily at Mac. "What authorities?" he asked softly.

Mac frowned. "What's that supposed to mean?"

After a long pause Nick got to his feet again and went to stand over Walt and Red. "If we bring in the police, there'll be an investigation. Publicity. Unpleasant publicity. Do we want that?"

Tracy scowled, wondering what he was driving at.

"What are you suggesting?" Mac asked, suddenly looking wary.

Nick shrugged. "Leave them. After about a week spent right where they are, they'll be ready enough to tell us everything—if the bears haven't gotten them."

"Good heavens, man," Lord Jon said. "You can't mean it!"

Red squirmed nervously. "Walt, maybe you oughta—"

"Shut up, Red," Walt said in a threatening tone.

Mac stroked his chin, appearing to give the suggestion serious consideration. "You have a point,

Nick. We wouldn't want the publicity. And you know what the police are up against when they try to interrogate prisoners. They have to follow so many idiotic rules, they never get to the bottom of things."

"Mac, surely you wouldn't leave them here in the bush for longer than a few hours!" Tracy said, hoping it was only a ploy.

"It's their choice," Nick said curtly. "If they don't want to give us answers, fine. We'll see how loose their tongues are after a few days and nights spent tied to this tree."

Tracy was aware that Nick and her grandfather were using scare tactics to get answers, but Nick's attitude toward her seemed to have reverted completely. Had the past days been a complete illusion? Had she kidded herself that Nick's feelings toward her had changed? Had she always seen a softness in him that just wasn't there?

At the moment he was unyielding, cold, and unemotional toward her as well as toward Red and Walt.

But earlier that morning hadn't Nick said he loved her? Perhaps she'd dreamed it. She wasn't sure. "You can't do this," she said, her voice shaky. "No matter what they've done, you can't leave them here." At this point she didn't know whether she really was arguing or just going along with their game.

"She's right," Red said enthusiastically. "You can't."

"They won't leave us for more than a couple of hours," Walt put in. "They'll call the cops and do everything by the book. They're what's known as decent folk."

Nick hunkered down in front of Walt and smiled. "And what gives you that idea? You think Bill MacKay could build a company like Sunstone by being a nice guy? And what about me? You figure I made it this far by following rules? We're no more decent than you, Walt. We're just smarter. We don't get caught." Rising and starting to pace back and forth, Nick raked his fingers through his hair. "We'll leave you all right. It's up to you whether it's here in the bush for a week or back on the lodge deck for a few hours."

"Look, we weren't gonna hurt nobody," Red offered. "Honest. We were only supposed to keep the girl until her granddad signed the papers."

"That's enough," Walt said in a warning tone.

"Papers?" Mac repeated. "Until I signed what papers?" He looked at Walt. "You'd better starting talking. I'm losing patience. Tell me exactly what's going on."

"I'll tell you nothing, old man," Walt said with a sneer.

Mac nodded, his eyes narrow, his jaw set in a hard line. "You win, Nick. Let's go." Turning on his heel, he started back toward the lodge.

"I say," Lord Jon remarked as he fell in step behind Mac. "One must credit that Cooper chap with loyalty. Imagine putting his life on the line this way. It seems there is honor among thieves after all."

"Honor!" Red shouted, finally snapping. "It ain't honor! Walt just wants the hundred grand he gets even if we end up in jail, which he figures we won't on account of the fancy lawyer we been promised if we need one. That's if we don't turn stool pigeon."

"Red, if you don't close your mouth," Walt began.

"You close your own," Red snapped, defiant at last. "What good's a lawyer and a stash of money if a bear eats us?"

Everyone had stopped dead and turned to look at the trussed-up pair.

"Well now," Nick said with a slight smile. "It looks as if Red has all the brains in your family after all. I'm surprised, Cooper. You actually believe that if you take the fall you'll get money? All that pay for a job you bungled? Don't you know the prisons are full of clowns who were promised the best legal help available if they played their cards right? What makes you think a person who would hire you for this kind of work would honor such a sucker's bargain?"

His pride stung, Walt lost his temper. "Because, smart boy, if she doesn't keep it, she knows I'll—" He stopped abruptly and cursed under his breath.

Tracy felt as if she'd been struck.

Nick turned to stare at her, his thoughts unreadable. "The one person I hadn't even thought of," he said, his voice taut with shock. He closed his eyes and took a deep breath to control himself, then looked at Tracy again. "And it was so obvious. So damned obvious right from the start."

Eleven

Tracy was paralyzed with the double shock of realizing who had hired Walt Cooper to kidnap her and seeing the dark anger in Nick's eyes. She swallowed hard, too stunned to say a word. Did Nick actually believe she'd plotted her own kidnapping for some twisted purpose?

"Walt, you might as well give us the name," Nick said quietly, his gaze fixed on Tracy.

"You're supposed to be the bright wonder boy," Walt shot back. "You figure it out."

"Yeah," Nick muttered. "I'm supposed to be the bright wonder boy. The company troubleshooter. I sure did a great job this time, didn't I?" Still looking at Tracy, he raised his voice slightly when he spoke to Walt again. "The name, Cooper. I think we've all figured it out, but why not make life easier for everybody? Who hired you?"

Tracy saw Walt's glance shift to her. When he smiled she was struck by the horrifying knowledge that he was actually going to say she was the one! She knew his accusation wouldn't hold water—but what if Nick believed him, even for a little while?

Her heart was hammering as she waited, wondering why her grandfather and Lord Jon were so silent. It was almost as if they were having doubts about her too. That was crazy! She was tired and upset and probably imagining things.

She hadn't imagined Walt's newest little game. "You're looking at her," he said at last.

Tracy's world began whirling. Nauseated by the feeling of vertigo, she suddenly realized how totally exhausted she was, how emotionally drained, how sickened by the fear that Nick might believe such a monstrous thing. Swaying slightly, she wanted to turn and run back into the woods, where she felt safe, where Nick had loved her—or had pretended to love her.

But all at once, without quite realizing how it had happened, she was in Nick's arms, cradled against his chest as he stroked her hair. "This guy's a joke, honey," he urged. "Don't let him upset you this way. Especially not now, sweetheart."

"Touching scene," Walt said, sneering.

Nick turned on him, keeping a firm arm around Tracy as he bit out each word. "Cooper, you've pushed your luck right to the edge, so start talking. I'm not a violent man, but right about now I'd like nothing better than to beat you to a pulp and leave you for the crows."

Confused and shaken, Tracy began trembling uncontrollably, hating her weakness yet unable to summon another shred of strength.

"Forget these two," Mac said abruptly. "We know

who's responsible, so why waste any more time? Let's go." He started off toward the lodge with Lord Jon right behind him.

Nick lifted Tracy as if she were weightless. "Don't worry," he told her almost under his breath as he carried her along the trail behind Lord Jon. "We'll send the police for these jerks. Is that what's bothering you? You're afraid we really are vengeful enough to make good on those threats?" He glanced back at Walt, then turned to Tracy again and winked. "It's tempting, I have to admit."

Tracy hardly could believe the tenderness in his expression as he looked down at her, the gentleness of his voice, the concern in his eyes.

"Walt, they're goin'," Red whispered. "They're really gonna leave us."

"Quite true," Lord Jon said pleasantly. "We're already dreadfully tardy, and Eleanor has planned a veritable feast for us. Freshly caught speckled trout. No one does trout with the special piquancy Eleanor gives it. A sprinkling of fresh wood sorrel is the secret, I believe."

"Come back here!" Red cried.

"Our garden has been particularly successful this year," Lord Jon went on. "And I swear Eleanor doesn't pick the vegetables until the water is boiling in a pot in the kitchen. We shall savor tiny new potatoes, or perhaps wild rice. And amaranth." He paused on the path and waved his arm like a full-blown Shakespearean player. " 'Silence and sleep like fields of Amaranth lie,' " he quoted, then smiled at Nick and Tracy. "From Walter de la Mare's 'All That's Past,' of course."

"Of course," Nick agreed, then raised a quizzical brow at Tracy. "Exactly what *is* amaranth anyway?"

"Pigweed," Mac supplied over his shoulder.

Lord Jon rolled his eyes and shook his head in dismay. "In some ways, Tracy, your grandfather is a Philistine. Nicholas, amaranth is a delightful green, related to lamb's quarters and rather like spinach in taste. Quite delicious the way Eleanor prepares it. You see, she—"

"Walt!" Red hollered as the little party disappeared into the bush. "They ain't bluffin'! They're leavin' us here for the bears an' goin' to eat their stupid pigweed! You gotta stop 'em!"

Still walking, Mac and the others listened carefully, but Walt remained stubbornly silent.

"Harlan!" Red screamed. "It was that Mrs. Harlan! *She* hired Walt. Come back here, you guys. Walt's gonna tell you everything, aren't you, Walt? About the papers an' . . . an' how we weren't to hurt nobody. Just throw a scare into 'em, right? You listenin' out there? You hear me? We wouldn't of hurt you guys! It wasn't even a regular kidnapping, see. We just had to hide the girl. Are you comin', somebody? Are you?"

Mac stopped, motioning the others to keep going. "I'll get the details and catch up with you. We can radio the police from Walt's plane." Suddenly he had a thought. "Jon, could you fly that newfangled aircraft? It'd speed things up if we could use the Cessna to hop over to your lake."

Lord Jon nodded. "Well, it isn't the *Queen Vicky*, but given a few moments to study the controls, I should think I can manage. I'm not completely unfamiliar with the newer models."

"The *Queen Vicky*?" Nick repeated.

"Lord Jon's plane," Tracy explained. "I could walk

now," she added, enjoying being in Nick's arms but beginning to feel a little silly.

"Hey!" Red screeched. "Help!"

Mac smiled and started to trace the path back to the prisoners, winking at Tracy on the way past.

"Really, Nick," she said, embarrassed. "I must be heavy."

He just held her a little tighter. "Lord Jon's a pilot on top of everything else?" he asked quietly. "And he has his own aircraft? So why did we travel by canoe?"

"Because, young man," Lord Jon said archly without looking back, "just as Mr. Cooper was unable to spot you by circling overhead, I should never have found you from the air."

"You can't leave us here!" Red wailed. "We didn't hurt nobody!"

"Stop your caterwauling!" Mac finally yelled. "I'm coming!"

Mac, Tracy, and Nick stood on the government dock in the small town waving to Lord Jon as he took off in his battered float plane and tipped the *Queen Vicky*'s wings in a cocky salute.

"Quite a man," Nick said, then laughed. "And quite a ride he gave us. I thought the flight in the Cessna to his place was an adventure, but from there to here? In that crate?" He shook his head. "Whew!"

Mac laughed and stepped between Tracy and Nick, casually draping his arms around their shoulders as the three of them walked over to the taxi that was waiting to take them to the local airport. "Jon learned to fly in planes like the *Queen Vicky*, and he got his lessons from the forestry service's pilots, the most

brilliant, dedicated, and insane bunch of fliers you'c
ever hope to meet. Be honest, Nick. Wasn't it fun?
All those loop-the-loops."

"Right," Nick said with an insincere smile. "Fun
The most fun I've had since the time I fell off a gian
roller-coaster. Luckily I managed to use my wind
breaker as a parachute."

"You fell off a roller-coaster?" Tracy asked. "When?
How did it . . . ?" She caught herself, then glared a
Nick. "You're getting to be as bad as Lord Jon and
Mac," she muttered.

"As bad?" Mac repeated. They'd reached the cab
and he stepped forward to open the rear door, mo
tioning to Nick to sit in back with Tracy. "Nick was
the one who started stringing Walt and Red along
about how we'd leave them for the bears. He almos
had *me* believing he meant it."

Nick waited for Tracy to get into the taxi, then
climbed in beside her, instinctively putting his arm
around her as he grinned up at Mac. "Does this
mean I'm a bona fide member of Leg-Pullers Anony
mous?"

"Bona fide," Mac told him, his eyes sparkling with
mirth.

Nick tested the water in the tub, then straight
ened up, satisfied. "All set," he called.

Tracy walked into the bathroom a moment later
her hair pinned in a loose topknot, her slender bod
wrapped in a pink terry-cloth robe. She smiled a
she saw the mound of bubbles, and breathed in th
fragrance of jasmine.

"It's not a northern lake, but it should ease awa

some of the aches and pains," Nick said as he reached for the belt of Tracy's robe and undid the knot.

"It looks wonderful," Tracy told him a bit breathlessly, excitement instantly welling up inside her. "You're spoiling me," she added in a husky whisper.

Parting her robe, he let his gaze linger on Tracy's pale loveliness. "No, love. I'm spoiling *me*."

Lazily Tracy let him help her shrug out of the wrap, closing her eyes to enjoy the tantalizing lightness of his hands as they slid over her shoulders and down her arms. "I'm so glad you're here," she murmured as he enfolded her naked body against his.

"Nothing could have kept me away from you," he said softly, his warm breath fanning her earlobe. "Not even Mac. You know, I was preparing all sorts of speeches during the entire flight to Chicago, wondering how a grandfather would take to being told his little girl wasn't under any circumstances going to sleep alone tonight."

Tracy's eyes opened wide. "You intended to say that?"

Nick trailed his lips over her smooth, round shoulder. "I had to be with you," he said between kisses. "And I couldn't be sneaky about it, so yes, I intended to say that." He raised his head and smiled down at Tracy. "But I didn't have to say anything. When we landed at Midway, Mac quietly asked me to spend the night here so you wouldn't be alone. And somehow I got the impression he didn't expect me to use one of the spare bedrooms."

"Shocking!" Tracy said with a laugh. "And I thought he was old-fashioned about such things. Did you also get the impression that Mac is doing a bit of not-very-subtle matchmaking?"

"Now that you mention it," Nick said as his lips traveled to the warm hollow at the base of Tracy's throat, "that was exactly my thought. Oddly enough, I didn't mind a bit." Tempted to brush his lips lower, to tease Tracy's responsive body to familiar peaks of need, he had to steel himself instead to set her away from him before he might strip off his own robe and take her right there on the floor. "You'd better climb into that tub before I forget you're here for a bubble bath," he warned, giving her a gentle push in the right direction.

Tracy tested the water with her toe, then submerged her body under the fizzing bubbles. As much as she wanted Nick, she was grateful for the bath. It was soothing to luxuriate in the pleasures of civilization. Besides, Nick was damp from his shower and smelled deliciously of soap and aftershave. She wanted to be as fragrant for him. "I wonder how Mac is doing," she said as she leaned against the back of the tub. "His energy is phenomenal, isn't it? After the stress he's been through, and then the tiring trip back home on top of it, he's gone to the hotel to greet shareholders at the cocktail party as if he had nothing more important on his mind. I feel guilty about not being there with him."

"He wouldn't hear of it," Nick reminded her as he sat on the edge of the tub, picking up the snifter of cognac he'd poured earlier. "He knows we're beat. Anyway, he said he'd just make an appearance, stay long enough to wave the flag and show that even a major scandal doesn't affect the smooth operation of Sunstone." He held the snifter out to Tracy. "Have a sip, sweetheart."

She inhaled the pungent fumes, then let Nick tip

the glass to her lips. "You think the scandal will break tonight?" she asked a moment later.

"Depends on how quiet the police are about taking Louise in for questioning, and on how quiet Louise is about going. Let's hope Mac got a chance to have his little talk with her beforehand. It's nice of him to warn her about what would happen." Nick shook his head, still amazed that Mac could be both clear-headed and compassionate enough to make as little fuss as possible in a difficult situation. "It's a whole lot better than Louise deserves."

"I'm not surprised," Tracy said. "Louise is Roy's widow. Somehow Mac feels he's doing his best friend's memory a disservice by turning her over to the police."

"He has no choice in the matter," Nick remarked. "Kidnapping isn't exactly a misdemeanor."

Tracy sighed heavily. "Poor Mac. Out of loyalty to Roy he'll help Louise all he can, even though he's never liked or trusted her. In fact, I think he blames her for Roy's heart attack. She's a very mean lady, you know. Domestic terrorist. Rules through temper tantrums, manipulation, phony girlishness, even an updated case of Victorian-style vapors if all else fails. I've seen her in action, and she's awful. What Roy saw in her even at the beginning I can't imagine. She's always been gorgeous, admittedly. Svelte, chic, still no silver threads among the gold, no wrinkles on her unfurrowed brow."

"Thanks to a lot of expensive repair work," Nick put in, too angry to be generous on the subject of Louise Harlan's much-vaunted beauty. Sick every time he thought of what the woman had tried to do to Tracy, he was in no frame of mind to joke about how well-preserved her looks were. Not for a moment did he believe she hadn't wanted Mac and Tracy harmed. Louise's insane plan to take control of Sunstone wouldn't have worked under any circumstances, but even she must have known her only chance of success was to get rid of the hostages permanently.

"I wonder if Hugh's in on this plot," Tracy said after a few moments. "I can't imagine he'd be *that* naive. Forcing Mac to turn over his shares to a numbered company? Expecting something like that to hold up legally once Mac was free to tell why he'd done it? Or even if—" She paused, unwilling to give voice to what she suspected would have happened to Mac, and to her, if Walt Cooper had been a more competent kidnapper. Instead, she went back to the question of whether Louise's son was party to the scheme. "After all, Hugh would have benefited from its success," Tracy said, thinking aloud. "I'm sure Louise had planned to make him chairman once Mac was out of the way." Tracy shook her head. "Louise always has been strange, especially when it came to her son's future." Tracy stopped abruptly as she saw how the hardness had returned to Nick's expression. But this time she simply was concerned, not frightened, not devastated by insecurity. She knew she'd misinterpreted Nick's reaction to Walt's blurted-out admission that a woman had hired him. "What's wrong?" she asked, sitting up and leaning forward.

"I should have seen what was coming," he said, holding the cognac snifter to Tracy's lips again as she took another sip. "When Louise looked at you, it was always with total hatred. If she so much as uttered your name, her voice dripped with acid. You're

everything her son isn't, and she can't stand that."
Nick closed his eyes, took a deep breath, and let it
out slowly, as if controlling a spasm of pain, then
belted back a swig of cognac. "Tracy, I was so damn
thickheaded. The night before we went to the lodge
for the retreat—the evening of the party here—I actually overheard Louise tell Cecil Berton and Hugh
that 'darling little Tracy' wouldn't be in their way
much longer. She added very hastily that she'd been
hearing rumors of an engagement between you and
that Trevor Gordon character." Nick scowled. "What
about him anyway? Were you and he an item? *Was*
an engagement imminent? I hadn't realized things
were ever that serious between you two."

Tracy completely forgot that Nick had been talking
about Louise's plotting. "They never were serious,"
she answered softly, delighted when he seemed relieved. "Trevor did ask me to marry him," she added,
wanting to be perfectly honest and rather liking the
flare of jealousy she saw in Nick's eyes. "I declined.
My affections, you see, already had been engaged
elsewhere."

Nick bent down to capture her lips in a kiss that
started out to be gentle but quickly became fiercely
demanding, its heat leaving her breathless and dizzy
and wanting more. Much, much more.

He cupped his hand behind her head and gazed at
her, his eyes troubled. "It drove me crazy to hear you
might marry that guy, Tracy. I wouldn't admit it to
myself though. Wouldn't admit I wanted you, was
fascinated by you, admired you. So there I was, too
caught up in a war with myself to notice that Louise
had warbled off that explanation *too* hastily, or that
it didn't make much sense, because even if you were

getting married, you still could be a potential successor to Mac. Alarms should have gone off full blast in my head, but they didn't. You were in the worst trouble possible, and I didn't anticipate it even when it was about to happen. I missed it all the way."

Tracy stared at him, finally understanding why he'd sounded so bitter earlier in the day when he'd realized the truth. He felt he'd failed. Failed her, failed Mac, failed himself. "Good heavens," she said lightly. "You'd need to be completely paranoid to see a takeover plot in what Louise said. You'd have to be as spaced-out as she is for such a goofy idea to cross your mind. Now, really, Nick, you know I'm right. You're being ridiculously hard on yourself."

He had to laugh, releasing her and sitting back. "When you put it that way . . ." His eyes suddenly grew dark with passion, his voice low and rich with desire. "Have you soaked enough in that bath yet?"

"Depends," Tracy said, scooping up two handfuls of bubbles and blowing them at him, her playful manner masking feelings almost too powerful for her to handle. "What did you have in mind?"

Nick's own emotions were running rampant, but he managed to rein them in. Smiling, he gave Tracy another sip of cognac, then with his free hand circled two fingers around the bubble-covered peaks of her breasts, lifting away enough of the foam to bare her shell-pink nipples, depositing a bit of froth on her nose and chin and cheeks. When she giggled, he bent to stroke his cheek over her face, feeling the bubbles pop against his skin.

"That tickles," Tracy said with a laugh. "I've heard of whisker rubs, but bubble rubs?" Reaching up to slide a hand inside his robe, she began exploring the coils of silky hair on the hard wall of his chest, discovering the muscles that rippled under his skin as if for the first time.

"So does that," Nick whispered, shuddering slightly at her tantalizing touch. He pleasured himself with her mouth, catching her lower lip between his teeth and nibbling gently, laving it with his tongue, sucking on it until it was ripe and swollen. Dipping one finger into the cognac, he smeared the warm liquid over her mouth and slowly licked it off.

Tracy's hands found the knot of his belt and undid it so she could push open his robe and tug on its sleeves, trying to get the barrier of cloth out of her way.

Nick set the cognac snifter on the edge of the tub, cupped both hands under Tracy's elbows, and raised her to a standing position. "Nice outfit," he said with a grin, his glance slowly perusing her bubble-clad form. "But I like you better naked, remember?" Inching his palms down over her body, he smoothed away the scented foam, leaving Tracy's skin glistening and totally exposed to his possessive gaze. Then, his hands on her waist, he lifted her high out of the tub and let her slide down against him.

"I—I'm all wet," she said when she was standing on the mat. "Now you are too."

Nick smiled and held her close, sharing his robe as he wrapped it around her.

Tracy snuggled contentedly against him, reveling in the sensation of skin touching skin, of her smooth, moist breasts being caressed by his silky chest hair. "I love you," she whispered. "I love you so much, there's no way I can ever tell you."

"You've already told me," Nick answered, holding

her closer, wishing he could absorb her body into his own so he would never have to be apart from her again. "You've told me in many ways, Tracy. And I hope you'll go on telling me, because I want to hear it. I'll never tire of hearing it. Or of saying how much I love you, sweetheart. Nothing else matters. I've found out that you're my top priority, my only real priority."

Tracy tilted back her head to look up at him, her thoughts suddenly troubled. "Nick, you're telling me something here. Or, rather, *not* telling me something. I know it. What do you mean, priorities? Why—"

He stilled her questions with a kiss that drove away all her worries. She was aware only of loving Nick and being loved by him.

At some point he'd flipped on the overhead heat lamp. Tracy felt warm from its penetrating rays, from the cognac, and most of all, from Nick's knowing caresses. Her body turned to liquid in his arms, until she was able to stand only because he held her.

At last she couldn't bear another second of the intoxicating, beautiful torture. "We finally have a bed at our disposal," she said raggedly. "Why don't we use it?"

Nick took her lips in another devastating kiss, at the same time lifting her in his arms and carrying her into her adjoining bedroom. Without releasing her mouth, he carefully placed her on the mattress that had been the scene of so many of her secret dreams of him, and proceeded to teach her how much sweeter reality could be.

Tracy was half asleep when her bedside phone rang. Nick picked it up and mouthed "Mac" when she looked questioningly at him.

He said little, mostly listening except for answering an occasional question. Nevertheless, Tracy pieced together from his expression and those few queries the gist of the conversation—until his last few cryptic responses.

"Yes, sir," Nick said, smiling. "Rest assured on that score. Definitely not. I wouldn't do that, sir."

Tracy had never heard him call Mac sir before.

"I know," he went on. "You can count on it, sir. I'm very serious. Soon you'll know exactly how serious. Now, can you get some sleep, Mac?"

Tracy frowned. What on earth were those two men discussing? "What was that all about?" she asked the instant Nick hung up the phone.

With his arm around her he absently stroked her breast. "Mac said the arrest was done so quietly, even the press didn't notice. He took Beryl aside and got her to prepare a statement that's already been handed out. The two of them fielded questions for a few minutes but basically managed to defuse the situation by meeting it head-on. By the way, he doesn't think Hugh knew what his mother was up to. Hugh was carping about the fact that you and I seemed to think we were above attending the annual meeting's social functions."

"Sounds typical of him," Tracy commented.

"And when Mac took him aside to tell him what was going down, Hugh apparently came close to passing out from shock. He's already offered Mac his resignation."

"Poor Hugh," Tracy said, cuddling against Nick's chest. "His mother kept him from being close to Roy, poisoning his mind from the time he was little. Now his mother has gone off the deep end."

"Count on one thing," Nick said. "Mac will help him in every way he can. Maybe Hugh will be better for all this. The corporate scene was never right for him. It was painfully obvious he was just trying to be the man his mother wanted him to be."

"The man his mother wished *she* could be, you mean," Tracy said. "Anyway, how did Mac sound? Tired?"

"Not a bit. Actually Mac sounds better than I've heard him in a while. He's finally on top again. That let's-be-considerate-of-poor-old-Mac garbage a few of the guys have been pulling lately had been undermining him, I guess."

"You noticed it too?" Tracy said, idly twirling a coil of Nick's chest hair around her index finger. "I resented the phony concern of those creeps so much, I wanted to punch their lights out."

Nick chuckled. "Violent little thing, aren't you? Remind me never to make you mad at me."

"Never," she repeated, wondering if the word implied the permanence she hoped for. Suddenly she remembered her curiosity. "What was that 'sir' stuff all about?"

Nick chuckled quietly. "It seems that Mac is pretty old-fashioned after all. He actually asked me if my intentions toward you were honorable."

Tracy smiled. "In those very words?"

"In those very words. He said he hadn't asked me to stay here with you so that I could add you to my list of—" Nick bit off his words.

Tracy finished the sentence for him. "Liaisons? Conquests?"

"Conquests," he mumbled. "But that was Mac's term, not mine. I don't have a list of conquests."

"What about Tanya?" Tracy asked impulsively.

Surprised, Nick laughed. "You remember Tanya?"

"Vaguely," Tracy lied, vividly recalling the statuesque body, the confident manner, the almond-shaped green eyes, the long, long legs . . .

"Tanya," Nick repeated, shaking his head. "A nice girl. She got married about two months after you met her—to an Australian sheep farmer."

"Tanya the Jungle Goddess, a sheep-farmer's wife?" Tracy blurted out, raising her head to stare at Nick.

"Jungle goddess?" he asked with a bemused smile. "What's that all about?"

"Nothing," Tracy mumbled, settling back into the crook of his arm. "What else were you and Mac going on about? What can he count on? What are you serious about? What did you mean, he'd soon know?"

"Not only a violent little thing, but nosy too." He clucked his tongue and rolled over until he was lying on top of her, his weight resting on his elbows as his body pinioned hers. "Never mind all that. Tell me again."

"I love you," she said readily. "I'm crazy about you. I adore you in every way a woman can adore a man." Her voice softened as she said it once more. "I love you, Nick."

He searched her azure eyes as if he needed confirmation, then smiled. "Do you love me enough to trust me?"

Instantly Tracy's antennae went up. Nick was planning something, and she had a strong feeling she wasn't going to like it. "I love you enough to . . . to love you even when I *don't* trust you."

"A little hard to follow but sincere," Nick said, laughing. "So you're saying you don't trust me?"

"Should I?" she asked.

He nodded. "Yes, Tracy. You should trust me. Always and forever, you should trust me. I promise I'll do only what's best for us."

Tracy raised her brow. "Really? Perhaps you might consider discussing with *me* just what's best for us? I have a vested interest, you know."

"In this particular case," Nick said after a moment's consideration, "there'll be no discussions." He was determined to be firm. "In this particular case you'll just have to—"

"Trust you." Tracy finished the sentence. Knowing she'd find out everything eventually and at that time deal with what Nick was up to, she temporarily conceded defeat. "Of course I trust you," she murmured with a mischievous, seductive smile.

Pleased by her surrender, his body stirred by her teasing invitation, Nick was quick to accommodate his lady's wishes.

Yet even as her softness welcomed him, her eyes luminous as she gazed up at him, her lips full and parted and inviting, he had the nagging feeling that Tracy's surrender to his firm stance had come a little too easily.

A moment later he didn't care.

Twelve

Nick strode purposefully into the office of the chairman of Sunstone Incorporated, hating what he was about to do but seeing no other choice.

Seated behind his huge teak desk, Mac glanced up, then he stood and thrust out his hand. "Glad you came straight to me as soon as you hit town," he said jovially, pumping Nick's hand. Motioning to the chair in front of the desk, he ignored the envelope Nick was carrying and barreled ahead as if nothing were amiss. "Sit down, Nick. I have news from the detective agency."

"Walt and Red?" Nick asked, settling into the comfortable black leather wing chair where he'd spent so many rewarding hours with Mac. It was hard to believe that particular episode was almost over. "Have those clowns been picked up again?" he asked, for the moment setting aside the reason for his visit. "I thought they'd headed straight from Canada to Mexico the minute they jumped bail."

"They did," Mac said, sitting back in his swivel

chair. "The detective I hired tracked them down in Tijuana—they're in jail."

Nick perked up. "They're in a Mexican jail? For what?"

"It seems that Walt decided kidnapping wasn't for him, so he tried a career move. A bad move, as things turned out," Mac went on. "He and Red were picked up by the Mexican authorities as they were about to take off for the States in a plane loaded with bales of marijuana."

Nick tapped his envelope on the arm of his chair and managed a tight smile. Under normal circumstances he'd have laughed at the fate of Cooper and his cousin, but he wasn't in a laughing mood. "So justice is served after all," he said quietly. "Which reminds me, what's the word on Louise?"

"Trial is set for next month. She's staying very quiet in the meantime, no bail-jumping for her. She's convinced she won't spend a day in jail, and I imagine she's right. She has top legal help and a battery of psychiatrists who are prepared to testify she's unstable at the very least."

"I'm sure she'll look like an angel for her day in court," Nick put in. "She'll turn on the charm and her grieving-widow number until there isn't a dry eye in the place. And she'll get away with everything."

Mac shook his head. "She's lost her social standing, she's going to endure public humiliation and ostracism, and she no longer has a stranglehold on her son. She's not getting away with anything, Nick."

Nick shrugged. "I guess you're right."

Deciding he couldn't wait any longer, Nick put the envelope on the desk in front of Mac.

"What's this?" Mac asked, opening the letter and quickly scanning it.

Nick rested his elbows on the arms of his chair and steepled his fingers, keeping his emotions under control though his stomach was in knots. He'd plunged into a deep melancholy as soon as he'd typed out the letter.

Mac tossed it aside. "Unacceptable," he stated flatly.

Nick blinked. "What did you say?"

"Unacceptable," Mac repeated, his gaze steady. "What would you expect me to say?"

"Mac, I don't like it either, but I have to resign. Surely you can understand why."

"As a matter of fact, I can't. Maybe you should try explaining."

Nick got up and began pacing, staring at the floor, his gray suitcoat open as he thrust his hands into the pockets of his trousers. "It's simple enough," he began. "I want to marry Tracy. I want to live with her here in Chicago and quit this miserable commuting she and I have had to do for the past weeks. It's no way to build a relationship. Anyway, that's getting away from the main issue. What counts is that I want to marry Tracy, and I'm fairly sure she wants to marry me. But I can't ask her as long as I'm with Sunstone." He stopped and glared at Mac, wishing he hadn't been forced to spell out the whole thing. "You see now?"

Mac smiled and shook his head. "Not really, Nick."

Nick raised his eyes to the ceiling and sighed explosively. With a deep breath he tried again, resuming his pacing, prowling Mac's office like a caged, hyperactive wildcat. "I always thought I was a pretty liberated guy," he confessed. "But I find I'm not. I can't marry a woman who ultimately could turn out to be my employer. On the other hand, I can't marry

the boss's daughter—granddaughter, in this case—as
a way to grab the brass ring. So in order to marry
Tracy, I have to leave Sunstone."

"To go where?" Mac asked calmly.

"I've had offers."

"Have you accepted any of them yet?"

"Not yet." Nick stopped pacing again and went to
lean on the edge of Mac's desk. "Look, I waited until
the flak over the kidnapping had subsided. I'll give
you all the notice you feel you need."

"Try forty or fifty years," Mac interjected. "Because
that's how long I need. That's how long Sunstone
needs. The president's office is vacant, Nick. I was
hoping you'd move in. It'd be a relief to me to have a
president who was more than a figurehead."

Nick straightened up and took another deep breath,
battling to remain calm. This resignation wasn't
going as well as he'd planned. "Tracy would be more
than a figurehead," he said at last. "Tracy has proven
herself a first-rate chief executive officer at Carlisle
Videos. Tracy is your president, Mac."

"Tell Tracy that," Mac said. "I'll be honest with
you, Nick. Tracy primed me for this confrontation.
She knew what you were planning. Why won't you
believe her when she says she doesn't want, has
never wanted, and will never want any part of Sunstone's head office?"

"Because she's willing to take a backseat for my
sake," Nick said. "Obviously she's no more liberated
than I am."

"Wrong on both counts. My granddaughter allowed
me to back Carlisle Videos, allowed her company to
be part of Sunstone, only on the condition that I
actively search for a potential successor to the chair

nanship. She's smarter—and more liberated—than
most people. Unlike Hugh, for instance, she refused
to take on a role that didn't fit her plans."

"And what are her plans?" Nick asked.

"That's a question you should ask Tracy," Mac
pointed out. "And when you do, be sure you listen
carefully to her answer. Then believe her. Tracy is
very truthful." Reaching into a desk drawer, Mac
brought out a document. "Read this," he said, handing his proud, stubborn protégé the thick sheaf of
papers. "Note the date and the fact that it's been
witnessed by my lawyer."

Nick unfolded the document. "Your will," he said,
then looked up and scowled. "Why would you show
me your will? I don't want to see this. I don't want
anything to do with your damn will."

"Read it," Mac ordered. "Sit down and read it
before I knock you down and read it to you."

Nick couldn't help grinning. The old Mac definitely had returned: tough, feisty, totally in control.
Okay, I'll read it," he conceded, returning to his
chair.

Several minutes later he looked up, stunned. "Dated
two years ago. A year after I joined Sunstone."

"Precisely," Mac agreed.

"You named me your successor back then?"

"With Tracy's blessing," Mac added.

Nick reread the clauses that had floored him most
of all. "Your shares? I'm to be given the option to
buy your shares from your estate, financing *from*
the estate if necessary? You expect me to believe
Tracy gave this clause her blessing too?"

"It was her idea," Mac said. "She could see all
sorts of conflicts and deadlocks if she, her mother,

and sister inherited the stock while the new chairman held only a minority position. With her inimitable charm, she said she'd rather have the money anyway."

Nick had to smile. He could just see the mischief in Tracy's eyes, the devilish grin she wouldn't be able to suppress when she made that kind of outrageous claim. "Why wasn't I told about all this?" he asked after several moments.

"I wanted you to stay because Sunstone was right for you, not because of some carrot dangling in front of your eyes."

"What if I'd left?"

"Wills can be rewritten," Mac pointed out. "I'd have been forced to give Tracy the unpleasant choice between taking on the role of successor herself or seeing it go to someone else—probably Cecil Berton."

Nick jumped to his feet and slapped the will down on Mac's desk. "Cecil Berton! You must be joking!"

"What do you care?" Mac asked gently. "You're prepared to walk away from the whole problem. All so no one can accuse you of marrying Tracy to get ahead. I didn't realize you were so worried about petty gossip, Nick. You surprise me."

Nick scowled. He hadn't looked at the situation from that perspective. "It's more than worrying about petty gossip," he protested. "It's—" He couldn't think of a single other reason for his concerns.

"It's what?" Mac prompted him. "If you're afraid *you'll* start believing you got ahead because of Tracy you're revealing a sorry lack of faith in my judgment. Remember, I chose you as my successor before you and my granddaughter so much as laid eyes on each other. I chose you because you're the best person for the job."

"Hell," Nick muttered. "Now I don't know what to think."

"Think about how you'll be leaving me in the lurch if you leave," Mac said quietly. "I need you, Nick. I was counting on turning a lot of my own load over to you." He leaned back, putting his hands behind his head. "I'd like to ease off a little, make the changing of the guard very gradual, start having some fun. I want to spend more time at the lake, maybe go prospecting with Jon. We know there's another big strike just waiting to be made, and all the signs point right to the area around Sunstone Lake. I feel the old fever coming on again, Nick, for the first time in decades. You wouldn't cheat an old geezer of a new lease on life, would you? Don't let me down. Don't let Tracy down." The famous blue eyes bored right into Nick's soul. "Don't let yourself down, son."

Nick stared at his boss, his mentor, his friend, then burst out laughing. "Mac, you're diabolical, you know that? I try to do what seems right and noble, and you turn it around so I feel as if I've been shamefully selfish."

"That's not diabolical," Mac said with a grin. "You *were* being shamefully selfish. But I forgive you. Now, how quickly can you get yourself moved over here? Mind you, there's no sense getting yourself an apartment right away. We'll put you up in the corporate penthouse until you and Tracy decide where you're going to live—unless you believe in long engagements?"

"It's been too long already," Nick said, beginning to get excited about the prospect of seeing Tracy every day instead of just on weekends, of holding her in his arms every night instead of settling for long phone calls. "And I haven't even asked her to marry me yet."

"Then hop to it, lad," Mac said cheerfully, tearing the resignation letter in half and tossing the pieces into the wastebasket. "Get a move on and ask her before she gives up on you!"

"I'll also ask," Nick said as he headed for the door, "about those plans of hers. The ones that are too important to let a mere corporate chairmanship get in the way."

"Plans?" Tracy asked.

"Plans," Nick repeated, refilling their champagne glasses as they sat at the white wrought-iron umbrella table in the lush English-style garden of Mac's mansion, where Nick had whisked the president of Carlisle Videos for an impromptu picnic.

She gave a delicate little shrug. "I just didn't want to become a corporate slave."

Nick lifted his glass and looked across the rim into the infinite sapphire depths of a pair of eyes he hoped would greet him every morning of his life. "Here's to your plans not to become a corporate slave. And to your beautiful eyes. And to how great you look in that neat little suit. Always wear that brilliant blue, honey. I'm crazy about that color on you."

She smiled. "Last week you told me always to wear bright red, and the week before that you insisted that green was my color. And—"

"Basically," Nick interrupted, "I like you best in whatever you happen to be wearing when I look at you. But I like you even better . . ."

"Better than best?" Tracy asked with a grin.

"Better than best," Nick insisted. "As you must be well aware by now, I like you better than best in whatever you happen *not* to be wearing when I look at you."

"The important thing is that you like me," Tracy said softly.

"The important thing is that I love you," Nick amended. "Now, about those plans. We've been so careful—*I've* been so careful—not to discuss the future. There are all sorts of things we don't know about each other. Why don't you want to be a corporate slave, Tracy?"

She felt a blush beginning at her throat and spreading upward. "There are things I want to accomplish with Carlisle Videos. Creative ideas to nurture and develop. New uses and applications of videos, for instance in education. Innovations I want to see carried on in our offices, like the company nursery for employees with children. Like flexible hours. Like profit sharing, job sharing—I want to keep putting my idealistic theories into action in the marketplace."

"What else?" Nick persisted, seeing Tracy's blush and suspecting he knew its cause.

She shifted uncomfortably in the white filigree lawn chair. "I guess I've always hoped I'd have children someday, and I want to be able to spend time with them."

Nick wasn't the least bit surprised. "You felt cheated because your mother had to work when you were little?"

"Not at all," Tracy said. "That's the point. Mom built up the chain of boutiques without sacrificing our home life. I could call her anytime, drop in to the

main store, where she worked, help out around
the shop—I could be with her. She could take time
off to see a school play or stay home when the chicken
pox hit. She wasn't in some high-powered meeting
behind closed doors, guarded by an army of secre-
taries. Mom was *there* for us. I want to be there for
my kids." She smiled, embarrassed by her outburst.
"If I do have any, I mean."

"Think we should?" Nick asked, swirling the
champagne around in his glass.

Tracy caught her breath. "I beg your pardon?"

"Do you think we should have children? After we're
married, of course. I'm kind of old-fashioned that
way. You will marry me, Tracy?" Putting down his
glass, Nick went to Tracy and dropped down to take
her hands in his, her eyes level with his, her lips
parted and waiting for his. "I won't become a corporate slave either, honey. Mac didn't, and since it
seems I'm to follow in his footsteps . . ."

"You are?" Tracy asked, relief washing through
her as she realized that Nick had either come to his
senses, or Mac had made him see things clearly.

"That appears to be the general idea," Nick told
her. "But I promise I'll always put us first, our family first—if we have a family. . . ."

"Oh, I'd *like* to have a family," Tracy said fer-
vently. "We'll take them up to Sunstone Lake and let
Mac teach them all the things he taught me—"

"Tracy," Nick interrupted, drawing her to her feet
as he straightened up. "Aren't you skipping over one
crucial detail?"

"Detail?" she repeated.

"Will you, Tracy Carlisle, take me, Nick Corcoran,
as your lawful wedded husband . . ."

Epilogue

Tracy sat behind her desk at Carlisle Videos and impatiently dialed the office of the president of Sunstone Incorporated, then swiveled in her chair to look down contentedly at the busy mid-afternoon traffic of the Loop. She was happy, happier than she'd ever been in her life, and not just because she loved early spring in Chicago. She loved any season in Chicago these days. Any season anywhere.

"Sunstone Incorporated," a pleasant voice said. "Mr. Corcoran's office."

"Mr. Corcoran, please," Tracy said.

"May I say who's calling?"

A new secretary, Tracy thought. Nick usually didn't have his calls screened. He was either available or not: No little games of corporate hide-and-seek for him. "It's his wife," Tracy said politely, making a mental note to ask Nick about a business matter. To ask her *husband*, she thought with a little thrill that hadn't gone away after more than two years of marriage.

"I'll see if Mr. Corcoran is in," the voice said.

"Hi, honey," Nick said after what seemed like an interminable wait. "Sorry I took so long. I was on another line."

Suddenly Tracy was incapable of speech.

"Honey," Nick repeated. "Are you there?"

"Hi," Tracy managed in a small voice.

"Hi," Nick said again.

There was a long pause while Tracy tried to decide where to start.

"Did you call for some reason, sweetheart?" he asked.

She nodded.

"Tracy?"

"Yes," she answered hastily. "I did. I called for a reason."

Another silence.

Nick tried prompting her a little. "Do you want to tell me what the reason is?"

"Well, I just got back to my office."

Nick waited for the rest. Nothing. "You just got back to your office," he repeated, not sure whether to worry or hope.

"Right," Tracy said. "A few minutes ago. But that's not what matters. It's where I was."

"Seeing the doctor?" Nick suggested, remembering her appointment, his heart beginning to pound. Was something wrong with her? Why did she seem to be in shock?

Tracy nodded again, then remembered Nick couldn't see her. The enormity of what she had to tell him was hitting her full force. In a way she didn't want to say it out loud, in case the whole thing turned out to be an illusion. Could anyone's life be as perfect as hers and be real? "You know the nursery here?"

"Yes," Nick said slowly, beginning to dare to hope.

"Well, you know who's going to be using it?"

The silence this time was at Nick's end of the phone.

Tracy smoothed her palm over her temporarily flat stomach, wondering how it was going to feel when there was movement in there, when her child and Nick's gave her a few forceful reminders of its presence.

Finally Nick spoke. "Did the doctor say how soon?"

"About seven months," Tracy answered. "At least, that's the estimate—" There was a click on the line.

Tracy hung up, sat back, and sighed, waiting. It was only about eight blocks from the Sunstone building to the complex where Carlisle Videos had its offices and studios.

Nick could make that in five minutes flat.

THE EDITOR'S CORNER

I feel envious of you. I wish I could look forward to reading next month's LOVESWEPTs for the first time! How I would love to sit back on a succession of the fine spring days coming up and read these six novels. They are just great and were loads of fun for us here to work on.

Starting off not with a bang but an *explosion,* we have the first novel in *The Pearls of Sharah* trilogy, **LEAH'S STORY,** LOVESWEPT #330, by Fayrene Preston. When Zarah, an old gypsy woman, gave her the wondrous string of creamy pearls, promising that a man with cinnamon-colored hair would enter her life and magic would follow, Leah insisted she didn't believe in such pretty illusions. But when handsome Stephen Tanner appeared that night at the carnival, she saw her destiny in his dark eyes and fiery hair. He found her fascinating, beautiful, an enchantress whose gypsy lips had never known passion until the fire of his kisses made her tremble and their sweetness made her melt. Leah had never fit in anywhere but with the gypsies, and she feared Stephen would abandon her as her parents had. Could he teach her she was worthy of his love, that the magic was in her, not the mysterious pearls? Do remember that this marvelous book is also available in hardcover from Doubleday.

Unforgettable Rylan Quaid and Maggie McSwain, that fantastic couple you met in **RUMOR HAS IT,** get their own love story next month in Tami Hoag's **MAN OF HER DREAMS,** LOVESWEPT #331. When Rylan proposes to Maggie at his sister's wedding, joy and fierce disappointment war in her heart. She has loved him forever, wants him desperately. But could he really be such a clod that he would suggest it was time he settled down, and she might as well be the one he did it with? Maggie has to loosen the reins he holds on his passion, teach Ry that he has love to give—and that she is the one great love of his life. Ry figures he's going to win the darling Maggie by showing he's immune to her sizzling charms. . . . This is a love story as heartwarming as it is hot!

From first to last you'll be breathless with laughter and a tear or two as you revel in Joan Elliott Pickart's **HOLLY'S**
(continued)

HOPE, LOVESWEPT #332. Holly Chambers was so beautiful . . . but she appeared to be dead! Justin Hope, shocked at the sight of bodies lying everywhere, couldn't imagine what disaster had befallen the pretty Wisconsin town or how he could help the lovely woman lying so pale and limp on the grass. When mouth-to-mouth resuscitation turned into a kiss full of yearning and heat, Justin felt his spirits soar. He stayed in town and his relationship with Holly only crackled more and warmed more with each passing day. But he called the world his oyster, while Holly led a safe life in her little hometown. Was love powerful enough to change Justin's dreams and to transform Holly, who had stopped believing in happily-ever-after? The answer is pure delight.

Next, we have the thrilling **FIRE AND ICE,** LOVESWEPT #333, from the pen—oops—word processor of talented Patt Bucheister. Lauren McLean may look serene, even ice-princess reserved, but on the inside she is full of fiery passion for John Zachary, her boss, her unrequited love . . . the man who has scarcely noticed her during the two or three years she has worked for him. When John unexpectedly gains custody of his young daughter, it is Lauren to the rescue of the adorable child as well as the beleaguered (and adorable!) father. Starved for ecstasy, Lauren wants John more than her next breath . . . and he is wild about her. But she knows far too much about the pain of losing the people she's become attached to. When John melts the icy barriers that keep Lauren remote, the outpouring of passion's fire will have you turning the pages as if they might scorch your fingers.

There's real truth-in-titling in Barbara Boswell's **SIMPLY IRRESISTIBLE,** LOVESWEPT #334, because it *is* a simply irresistibly marvelous romance. I'm sure you really won't be able to put it down. Surgeon Jason Fletcher, the hospital heartbreaker to whom Barbara has previously introduced you, is a gorgeously virile playboy with no scruples . . . until he steps in to protect Laura Novak from a hotshot young doctor. Suddenly Jason—the man who has always prided himself on not having a possessive bone in his body—feels jealous and protective of Laura. Laura's pulse races with excitement when he claims her, but when a near accident shatters her com-
(continued)

posure and forces long-buried emotions to the surface, grief and fury are transformed into wild passion. Danger lurks for Jason in Laura's surrender though, because she is the first woman he has wanted to keep close. And he grows desperate to keep his distance! Jason has always got what he wanted, but Laura has to make him admit he wishes for love.

We close out our remarkable month with one of the most poignant romances we've published, **MERMAID**, **LOVESWEPT #335**, by Judy Gill. In my judgment this story ranks right up there with Dorothy Garlock's beautiful **A LOVE FOR ALL TIME**, LOVESWEPT #6. Mark Forsythe knew it was impossible, an illusion—he'd caught a golden-haired mermaid on his fishing line! But Gillian Lockstead was deliciously real, a woman of sweet mystery who filled him with a joy he'd forgotten existed. When Gillian gazed up at her handsome rescuer, she sensed he was a man worth waiting for; when Mark kissed her, she was truly caught—and he was enchanted by the magic in her sea-green eyes. Both had children they were raising alone, both had lost spouses to tragedy. Even at first meeting, however, Gillian and Mark felt an unspoken kinship ... and a potent desire that produced fireworks, and dreams shared. Gillian wanted Mark's love, but could she trust Mark with the truth and shed her mermaid's costume for the sanctuary of his arms? The answer to that question is so touching, so loving that it will make you feel wonderful for a long time to come.

Do let us hear from you!

Warm regards,

Carolyn Nichols

Carolyn Nichols
Editor
LOVESWEPT
Bantam Books
666 Fifth Avenue
New York, NY 10103